A TOUCH
OF LOVE

Patricia Hagan

A KISMET™ Romance

METEOR PUBLISHING CORPORATION
Bensalem, Pennsylvania

PATRICIA HAGAN

Patricia Hagan is the New York *Times* bestselling author of twenty published novels. A former award-winning TV-Radio Motorsports journalist, she and her husband, Erik, reside atop a North Carolina mountain with their wire-haired fox terrier, Krystal. Her hobbies are reading, painting, and hiking.

ONE

Kelly had just finished her swim across the cove and back but was not yet ready to climb up on the pier. She preferred just to tread water, a little ways out, and watch the others gathered beyond, on the deck of the cabin at the top of the rise. She wondered again what was going on. Everyone was acting as though they knew a secret she didn't. Oh, not that it was all that annoying. Not at all. Just sort of perplexing. She liked Neil's friends, two couples he'd known since college days. They'd made her feel welcome in their social clique since day one, nearly six months ago, when she and Neil had begun dating.

They had gathered at Neil's parents' cottage on Lake Norman, about an hour's drive north of Charlotte. The others had been able to arrive Friday evening, but at the last minute, Kelly had to take emergency duty when one of the other veterinarians became ill. She'd also had to take his place staffing the clinic all day. So she had not arrived till around five o'clock, and from the minute she stepped out of her Bronco she had sensed something was in the air. The guys, Larry and Chad,

had knowing grins plastered on their faces while their wives, Brenda and Vickie, kept exchanging conspiratorial smiles. Maybe, after all their years of trying, one of them was at last pregnant, but if that were so, Kelly couldn't figure out why they simply didn't tell her. What was the big deal? She'd be glad to share their happiness.

She saw Neil leave the deck and head down the slope in her direction. She climbed up the ladder, began to dry off with the towel she'd left there.

"Honey, I wish you wouldn't swim alone." He kissed her cheek, held out a frosty bottle of beer he'd brought for her.

She waved it away, saying, "You know I'm on call." She also started to remind him there was no point anywhere in the tiny cove where the water was over her head, but she let it go.

"One beer won't hurt. As hard as you've been working lately, you deserve it."

She could see the hint of disapproval mirrored on his face as they stood there in the peachy glow of the late June sunset. The air was warm, still, and the only sound, the gentle hum of the water mosquitos hovering just above the calm surface of the lake.

"Come on." He pushed the beer at her again. "Relax. It's going to be a wonderful evening, and you're tense. I can tell."

She offered a patronizing smile, made her tone gentle, pleasant, though inside she felt agitation. "The only tension I feel, Neil, is at times like this when I have to justify myself. I don't drink anything when I'm on call. Period. Who wants to bring in their sick pet to a veterinarian with booze on her breath? What kind of credibility does that give me?"

He shrugged, tipped the bottle to his lips instead, took a swallow before saying, "I wish I'd known sooner you were on call. We could've made it another weekend.''

''That couldn't be helped. I didn't know till the very last minute.'' She started to walk on up the pier.

He fell into step beside her. He and the others had spent the afternoon water skiing. He'd taken a shower and changed into crisp khaki shorts, a bright Alexander Julian sports shirt, worn brown leather dockers. Deeply tanned, Neil looked fit, healthy, his body toned from afternoons playing racquetball or tennis.

Kelly found him extremely handsome, with his thick, curly black hair and hazel eyes. He was charming, intelligent, and very successful. Already he was a vice-president of one of the state's largest banks and not yet thirty.

Considered one of Charlotte's most eligible bachelors, Brenda and Vickie had confided to her how they'd introduced Neil through the years to every single one of their unmarried sorority sisters or any other unattached girl they felt might be suitable for him. Always, after a few dates, he lost interest. When they reminded her she now held the record—nearly six months—Kelly would bite her tongue to keep from making a sarcastic retort like *''Gee, lucky me!''* She had to admit she liked Neil, a lot, but good grief, she didn't like feeling she was competing for a prize, trying to set a Guinness world record or something. Besides, she was definitely not anxious for any kind of commitment. Not for a long, long time. There were too many cobwebs in the past that had to be swept away. The past years had been filled with turmoil and conflict, and there were many fences to mend—especially with her parents.

Neil reached to take her hand, nuzzled the back of her neck with his lips, and whispered, ''I can't wait to get you all to myself tonight. God, you drive me crazy in a bikini.''

His hand slipped to caress her bare hip, and she felt a rush of desire. Sex with Neil was good, but she had to admit it could be better. There were times when she wanted more, wanting him to touch her in special places, try different things. But he always took the lead, as though he were the star in a play, and she merely the supporting actress, to be led step by step all the way through the drama. Afterwards, she would be angry with herself for not taking the initiative, then rationalized she would become bolder as time went by. Yet it bothered her terribly that this was the first relationship in her life when she'd been hesitant to *be* bold, to make known what *she* wanted in bed. And why? Were the cobwebs of the past affecting *that* part of her life, too?

As they approached the deck, Kelly took note of the way all conversation immediately ceased. Finally, curiosity got the best of her, and she whispered to Neil, "What's with everybody tonight? I get the feeling something's going on I don't know about."

"You're imagining things." He gave her a playful push in the direction of the cabin, grinned, and winked. "Hurry and change."

She went into Neil's room, where they slept together on weekends his parents weren't around. Other times, she had the guest room. No matter they were both mature adults in their late twenties, he said there was no need to personify the sexual side of their relationship. Okay, fine. She'd play by the rules in his parents' home, just as she yielded to her own in theirs.

She stripped out of her bikini and stepped into the shower, thinking about all the nights she slept over at Neil's townhouse. He lived in the same expensive complex as Larry and Brenda and Chad and Vickie. He'd hinted a few times that she might as well move in, that they could live together, but he never responded to her challenge of "What's the difference in living together and sleeping in the same room at your folks' cabin?"

Once, he had jovially accused her of being a rebel, and she wondered if he were really teasing or if he'd got that from his mother, Dodie. She and Kelly's mother, Verna, seemed to stay on the phone to each other when they weren't lunching or playing golf at the country club. Yet Kelly doubted her mother would have told Dodie everything. She was too embarrassed over what she described as Kelly's past *nonconforming* and *mutinous* behavior.

Stepping into the shower, the past came raining down along with the water. Her mother had nearly died giving birth to her, could not have other children, had never let Kelly forget that fact. So whenever she had done anything to displease, Verna reminded Kelly of her extreme sacrifice and suffering. Accordingly, Kelly had begun to revolt at an early age, determined her life was her own, that her reason for being was not to make up to her mother for pain and anguish suffered in child-birth. She wanted to be herself, do her own thing, and Verna couldn't accept that kind of independence. They locked horns constantly. In grammar school, Kelly had driven her crazy with her tomboy antics, refusing to play with dolls and take piano lessons and all the other lovely "little girl" things Verna wanted. In high school, she hadn't wanted to be a cheerleader or a majorette. She liked sports and excelled, becoming the star center on the basketball team and a record-setter in track.

But the big blow-up had come when she was in her first year of medical school, because suddenly, after all the years of hard work, Kelly began to have self-doubts. Did she really want to be a doctor? Was that *her* dream . . . or her *parents'*? When Jackie Lancaster, her roommate from England, invited her to go home with her for spring break, Kelly jumped at the chance. She desperately wanted, needed, a break in routine and scenery to sort out her confusing thoughts.

Jackie's father was a veterinarian, with a busy practice in a rural section outside London. At once, Kelly became fascinated and was soon hanging around in his clinic and going with him on large animal calls. By the time her visit was over, she'd made up her mind. She wanted to be a veterinarian! She had always loved animals, anyway, and decided ministering to God's four-legged creatures was her true calling.

When she returned home to announce her plans, her mother had gone to bed with one of her asthma attacks she claimed was brought on by stress. In just the little while Kelly had been in pre-med, she had concluded the *attacks* were psychosomatic but kept her mouth shut. Her father was a pharmacist, an intelligent man, and if he couldn't see through her, Kelly was not about to try to make him.

She applied for admission to the state school of veterinary medicine in Raleigh and was accepted. Her mother was so angry she said there'd be no more money for her education. Her father, Walter, ever the marshmallow, stood with her, though Kelly suspected he thought Verna was carrying things a bit far. But *his* mother, Edie, had come through for Kelly. She was quite wealthy, said she'd finance her schooling, and there was nothing Verna could do but pout. She and Edie had never gotten along, but she avoided confrontation due to anticipation of the day Edie passed on, and she would then have control of all her money, since Walter was an only child.

The change in dreams caused a breach in the family, however. Kelly felt positively alienated from her parents. She could look back now and see that was what made her so vulnerable to Len Barfield. He was a student in the college of liberal arts, and after a whirlwind romance of only a few weeks, they eloped.

Verna had another asthma attack because Len was everything she did *not* want in a son-in-law. From a poor background, he was going to college on a student loan she predicted Kelly would wind up repaying. He was also somewhat of a leftover from the sixties, with long hair, clothes straining for the rag barrel, thong sandals. He also drove a beat-up Chevy van painted with peace symbols.

Even Edie was upset with Kelly this time. "It's just your way of rebelling against your parents *again!*" she accused.

But Kelly denied that, saying she and Len really loved each other. And she believed that, too, or tried, anyway. Within a year, he'd dropped out of school and gone to work in a vegetarian bar. They were living in a trailer, which was always overflowing with his free-loading friends. Kelly's patience, and love, was stretched to the breaking point, and the snap came the day she came home from class early and found him naked in bed with a waitress from the bar smoking clove cigarettes. She had sent a lamp smashing against the wall and screamed for him to get out and take "Miss Tofu" with him and never come back. He did—and he didn't—and that was the end of their brief and stormy marriage.

Verna had had a field day of "I-told-you-so's" and "See-what-happens-when-you-marry-out-of-your-class" with a few "That's-what-you-get-for-not-marrying-a-rich-man!" thrown in for good measure. Kelly passed on Christmas holidays that year so she wouldn't have to listen to it. She also went to school year round, more to avoid her parents than to finish early.

Upon graduation, she'd felt the offer from the Charlotte clinic was an omen. After all, she was tired of estrangement from her parents, realized she was desperate to feel a part of them. No matter she did not *like* them, she had never denied *loving* them.

When she'd made her announcement, for the first time since her decision to become a vet, Verna was actually pleased. She also wanted peace, happily proclaiming, "We're going to be a real family, at last!" She had then busied herself redecorating the room above the garage so Kelly could have some privacy, for it was understood, of course, she would move home and be a family member until she became established, and, Verna not-so-shyly hinted, eventually married a nice man and presented them with lots of grandbabies. Kelly wasn't so keen on living at home but decided to go along to get the ball rolling to smooth things over. Later, she could ease into a place of her own.

Verna had wasted no time in getting Neil and Kelly together. Neil happened to be the son of Verna's old college roommate, Dodie Hamilton, now Mrs. *Doctor* Gregory Brandon. "Frankly, I was ashamed to introduce you before, even though I knew they'd moved to Charlotte for Gregory to take the position as Chief Surgeon at the new hospital," she had told Kelly in her usual brusque manner. "He wouldn't have looked at you twice, the way you were behaving, but now that you seem to have come to your senses, I think the two of you would be perfect for each other. And I don't mind telling you nothing would please me more than to see my daughter married to Dodie Brandon's son."

Kelly had been dubious, leery, anything but enthused over anyone her mother had in mind for her, and it had come as quite a shock to discover Neil was nice. Very nice. They seemed to click from day one. Yet, as their relationship had developed, progressed, she felt something was missing—something she couldn't figure out, and it was needling her more and more.

Turning off the shower, along with the flood of memories, Kelly dried herself. Then she dressed in shorts and a blouse. Her hair was still damp, so she pulled it back in a pony tail.

The minute she went out on the deck, conversation once more came to an abrupt halt. Larry and Chad were smirking, and Brenda and Vickie giggled.

Kelly took a deep breath of resignation. If they wanted to play games, fine.

Brenda pointed to the beeper she'd tucked in her hip pocket. "Will that thing really work way out here?"

Before Kelly could say anything, Neil interjected, "God, I hope not!"

Kelly ignored him, answering Brenda, "It probably won't, but the answering service has the phone number here just in case."

"Then let's take the phone off the hook," Neil brightly suggested, even though he knew she'd never agree.

She gave him a withering look that said, "Don't-you-dare!" He got that message loud and clear, laughing to let her know he was only teasing, then said, "Okay, let's put the steaks on. I'm starved."

"When are we going to have the champagne?" Brenda asked Neil with another mysterious giggle.

He responded, "Now that Kelly is here, we'll open a bottle soon."

"None for me, thanks," Kelly said, unaware of the worried look Brenda was giving Neil behind her back. She helped herself to the spread of delicious hors d'oeuvres the girls had prepared—shrimp, hot wings, clam dip, and teeny little cheese and mushroom quiches.

"You have to have one glass," Brenda said, with a wink in Neil's direction.

Kelly shook her head. "No can do."

Neil frowned. "Tonight is a special occasion, Kelly. You can have *one* glass, for heaven's sake."

"Nope." She was not going to argue about it.

Brenda gave a dramatic sigh, thought of all the girls she'd introduced to Neil and couldn't resist pointing out, "That's what you get for getting involved with a *veterinarian*, Neil."

"That's right, Neil," Kelly impishly goaded, giving him a playful bump with her hip. "If you'd fallen for one of those lady wrestlers they introduced you to, she'd drink everybody under the table."

They all had to laugh at that, and the tension was eased just a bit.

Soon, the steaks were sizzling over charcoal, foil-wrapped baked potatoes to one side. Crisp green salads were placed on the redwood picnic table. A half moon was rising over the pines, and the lake shimmered in its silvery light.

Neil watched Kelly as she talked and laughed with his friends and thought once more what a wonderful wife she was going to make. He had to admit when his mother had first suggested he call the daughter of her college roommate and ask her out, he'd groaned inwardly. Then, after asking around and finding out that Kelly Sanders was a veterinarian and a divorcee, he groaned *outloud*. His impression of a female vet *was* about the same as a lady wrestler. He also wasn't keen on getting involved with someone with a painful past. So he told his mother to please forget it. Then, one night he'd gone home for dinner to walk in and find Kathleen Turner's twin having a cocktail in his mother's living room. Tall, willowy, hair the color of gold dust, and smoky eyes fringed with thick lashes, combined with a sensuously husky voice—he was hooked then and there. Not only was she gorgeous, but she was also witty and high-spirited and more fun to be with than any girl he'd ever known. He made up his mind she was the one he'd been looking for and would ultimately marry.

Everything had progressed nicely in their romance, he felt, till he decided it was time to get serious. Then she'd turned cool, changed the subject. He knew her parents wholeheartedly approved of him as a son-in-law. Verna Sanders had invited him for a private lunch one day to confide that fact, as well as make suggestions as to how he could best handle Kelly's rebellious spirit. Marriage, he felt, would take care of that. Once she shared a life with someone else, he was confident she'd lose some of her independence. He had also earned big brownie points with Verna by assuring her he'd do everything possible to influence Kelly to give up practicing vet medicine and settle down to being just a wife, mother, and homemaker—the answer to Verna's prayers for her daughter's future.

Neil felt that because of her divorce Kelly would continue to evade any discussion of marriage. That, however, had merely been a reckless act of defiance during a difficult period of her life, as Verna had put it. All Kelly needed was guidance and manipulation into understanding that one mistake with the wrong person did not mean she could not find happiness with the right person. So, after intimate conferences with his mother and Verna, he reached the conclusion that the only solution was to jolt Kelly into realizing she *did* want to marry him.

He had planned it all out carefully. Larry and Chad already had their cars packed so they wouldn't be staying that night, leaving them to their privacy once the engagement was official. Weeks ago, Verna had sneaked Kelly's birthstone ring to him so he'd be sure to size her diamond correctly. Two bottles of Kristal were chilling. The ring was in his pocket, ready to be slipped into Kelly's glass when it was refilled. She would see it sparkling amidst the bubbles, and he knew that at that particular instant, she'd never be able to say no. The extra touch, he felt, was being able to celebrate such an auspicious occasion with their friends.

Chad called from where he hovered at the grill, "Hey, I think these are ready. Somebody get a platter."

Kelly was closest to the kitchen and said she'd oblige. The second she was gone, Brenda and Vickie converged on Neil to ask how he was going to handle things if she wouldn't drink. Wasn't the idea to make merry, get her mind on other things, so she'd be absolutely astonished to find the ring glittering in her refill? He said not to worry. "I'll just put it in her glass to start with. All she has to do then is see it."

Vickie squealed. "I think it's so romantic. You know, Chad put my ring in a box of candy, mashed it right down into a chocolate covered cherry! I remember thinking he was crazy, insisting I eat that piece when it was so messy."

Brenda chimed in with her nostalgic tale of how Larry had placed her ring on top of a hot fudge sundae. "But I think Neil's idea is the greatest yet. So romantic."

Neil beamed. He'd promised himself long ago to outdo his buddies and couldn't wait to reveal how he'd outdone them on honeymoon plans, as well. Larry and Brenda had gone to France. Chad and Vickie had opted for a cruise on the QE II. He'd topped them all; he planned to lease a yacht for a cruise around the Greek islands. Of course, that was a long way off. Verna and his mother had made it clear they wanted ample time to plan the most lavish wedding Charlotte, North Carolina, had ever seen. Fine. He could wait. He'd sure waited long enough to find the girl of his dreams, anyway, and now he just wanted to make it official that Kelly Sanders was going to be his wife!

Kelly came out with the platter, and, smiling mysteriously once more, Neil headed inside as he called over his shoulder, "I'll get the glasses and the champagne."

Kelly started to remind him she didn't want any but decided not to waste her breath. If he poured, she just wouldn't drink. God, why was he being so persistent?

Neil got out a tray, six champagne glasses, then opened the first bottle. There was a pop, the hiss of rising wine, and then he filled each glass. Finally, he took the huge, pear-shaped diamond from his pocket and dropped it into the glass he would set before Kelly. Once more, he felt a glow of pride at his taste. The ring was exquisite. No matter the price. Nothing but the best for the future Mrs. Neil Brandon.

Unable to keep the excited tremor from his voice, he called to no one in particular, "Get the door!"

Vickie was closest, leaped to oblige. She saw the ring, sparkling in the crystalline bubbles and could not suppress an impressed gasp. Neil scowled at her, pursed his lips in a reminder for her to be silent.

Kelly was probing at her steak with her fork, anxious to see if it was cooked the way she liked—pink, but not bloody. She was oblivious to all the tittering around her.

With great flourish, holding the tray high, so Kelly could not see the glass with the ring in it from where she sat, Neil announced, "This is a very special occasion. We are about to have a toast, and I'd like everyone but Kelly to stand."

Kelly looked up then, blinking in confusion. Why wasn't she supposed to stand? She'd take a sip, for crying outloud, to be sociable. No big deal. She started to get up with the others, but Neil juggled the tray with one hand, while gesturing wildly for her to remain seated. "No, don't get up. Sit there. I've got a special glass for you, and—"

The phone rang.

Everyone but Kelly groaned in unison.

Neil had just glanced at his watch, knew it was not yet eight o'clock. Dodie and Verna had made it plain they'd be chewing their nails wanting to hear all the details of how Kelly had reacted when she saw the ring. He'd made it clear they should wait till nine, at least, but they were so excited, they probably hadn't been able to wait till then. Kelly's mother was even hosting a champagne brunch the next day for both families to celebrate. Now, however, they were spoiling everything. "Let it ring!" he snapped irritably.

Kelly was on her feet at once. "I can't do that, Neil. It might be the answering service." She rushed inside, leaving him amidst worried and sympathetic looks from his friends.

It was, indeed, the answering service, and Kelly was informed she was needed at the farm of Joe Winters. A mare was having a difficult time foaling. She had the necessary large animal instruments in a bag in her Bronco, told the service to get back in touch with Mr. Winters and let him know she was on her way. "It should take me about a half hour to get there from where I am."

She hung up, rushed back outside to quickly offer obligatory regrets.

Everyone was gathered around Neil, who was standing facing her direction, still holding the tray in his hands. Kelly was struck at once by the almost accusing and angry looks on everyone's face, mingled with the disbelief and near horror mirrored on Neil's. She desperately wanted to know, once and for all, what the hell was going on here tonight, but there just wasn't time. "Sorry, but I've got to go. I've got to help deliver a colt, and—" She froze!

She had seen the ring.

TWO

Kelly never ceased to find the miracle of birth a hallowed experience. And, as she knelt beside the mare, tears of joy streamed down her face.

It had been a long night and now, through the barn window, she could see the first watermelon fingers of dawn starting to creep upwards from the eastern horizon.

When she'd arrived at Joe Winters' farm the night before, a quick examination of the mare revealed there was no real problem. She was, indeed, in labor, but these things could not be rushed. As it turned out, the reason for her prolonged efforts turned out to be not one fuzzy, wobbly-legged colt—but *two*. Kelly had never delivered twins before, and the event had left her a bit shaken. It was truly moments like this when she felt so warm and happy inside that her reasons for choosing veterinary medicine were reinforced.

Joe Winters stood just outside the stall. Shaking his head, he murmured again, "I just can't believe it. Twins. Never dreamed she was gonna foal twins. They look healthy, too."

"*Very* healthy," Kelly assured. "I don't see anything to worry about. Your mare is fine, too."

"I sure do appreciate your stayin' out here all night, doc. I mean, once you knew what was goin' on, there weren't no need, but I'm beholdin' to you all the same. If somethin' had gone wrong, I doubt I'd have known what to do."

"Twins can be tricky," Kelly pointed out. "Sometimes you think it's going to be a breech and start trying to turn things around, and then complications set in. I was glad to stay." *He didn't know how glad,* she thought, recalling those last embarrassing moments at the cabin.

She put away the last of her instruments, closed the big leather bag, and stood. Every bone in her body was aching, it seemed, and she was so sleepy her eyelids felt like sandpaper. It was still a good half hour drive back to the clinic, where she'd need to check the sick animals there before going home, hopefully to sleep the rest of the day.

"The missus is fixin' some ham and biscuits." Joe followed her out of the barn.

Kelly could smell the wonderful aroma of country ham sizzling and fresh-brewed coffee all the way from the farmhouse. It was tempting, but she needed to be on her way. "Thanks, but I've got things to do. Call if you have any problems or questions."

He thanked her again. She tossed her bag into the back of the Bronco, got in, and was soon on her way down the dusty road headed for the interstate that would breeze her back into Charlotte. She was not about to return to the lake, even though she'd half-heartedly promised Neil she would so he would stop arguing and she could get away.

She shuddered to remember the nightmare. Seeing that diamond ring in the glass of champagne had rendered her speechless. All the pieces of the puzzle had suddenly fit together, there in that moment when time stood still. The way everyone had been acting, Neil's insistence on having champagne, his mysterious behavior the past few days—it all added up to the horrifying reality that he'd chosen that particular way to propose.

But why?

Kelly's teeth ground together so hard her jaws ached, and she knew how it must feel to be shoved into a corner with no way out except to come out fighting. They had never spoken of marriage! True, there'd been several times, especially lately, when Neil had tried to talk of serious things, like how he didn't want her to see anybody but him, assuring *she* was the only girl in *his* life, wanting to know how *she* really felt about *him*. But she just hadn't wanted to talk about it, had tried to explain her feelings that they should just relax, enjoy the present, let the future take care of itself. Now it was obvious he'd been much more serious than she imagined, and when she'd continued to dodge and duck the issue, he decided to force it. And it made her absolutely livid with rage to think how he had to have thought if he put her on the spot, in front of his friends, she'd never have the nerve to refuse.

"Well, guess again, *bucko!*" she muttered outloud, clenching the steering wheel so hard her knuckles turned white. She wasn't about to be manipulated into marrying Neil or anybody else.

When she had continued to just stand there, frozen, staring at that huge diamond, Brenda had finally giggled and commanded, "Well, go on! Scoop it out, Kelly, and let's see it on your finger. It's beautiful."

"Yes!" Vickie had chimed in to urge. "Get it out."

Slowly, Kelly had got hold of herself, finally managed to shake her head as she backed away from the glass as though, instead of a pear-shaped diamond engagement ring, it were a vicious tarantula glaring out at her. "No," she'd choked out her protest. "I . . . I've got to go. Emergency . . ." And, at last, she was able to command her trembling legs to move, take her quickly out of the cabin, breaking into a run across the lawn to the waiting Bronco.

Neil had set the tray down and caught up with her as she was about to back out of the driveway. Looking absolutely wretched, he had cried, "You can't just leave like this, Kelly. We have to talk. I love you, and—"

She had bit out the words, fury overtaking surprise. "How could you do this to me? You never asked me if I wanted to marry you!"

He pleaded with his eyes. "But you knew I loved you, and I assumed—"

"*Assumed?*" she had screeched in echo. "Oh, come on, Neil. Grow up! You don't *assume* things like that. You don't just go out and buy somebody an engagement ring and present it in front of your friends without asking lots of questions first. I feel like a fool."

He had hung his head. "Think how *I* feel."

"You deserve it! It's all your fault. You should've asked me, Neil, and I'd have told you I don't want to marry you."

At that, his own ire exploded. "Well, *I* happen to love you, Kelly, and when you love somebody as much as I love you, it's only natural to want to get married."

"But you're supposed to find out how the other person feels before you create a production number that leaves everybody feeling like idiots!"

He had blinked as the thought suddenly occurred. "You mean you really don't love me?"

She had sighed, impatiently gunned the motor, thought how if he didn't get out of her way in about ten seconds, she'd have to floorboard it and leave him standing there feeling like an even bigger fool in a cloud of dust, and she hadn't wanted to hurt his feelings anymore than she already had. "I *like* you, Neil. I'm not so sure about love. Not yet. I'm just getting my life back together, building a career, and—"

"But you don't *need* a career," he had argued, "except as my wife, and—"

"We'll have to talk about this later. I've really got to go. I'm sorry about the way things turned out, for your sake, but it's not my fault. I never led you on in any way to give you the impression I'd put that ring on my finger."

"Will you come back as soon as you've finished? So we can talk?"

"Maybe . . ." she had pressed down on the accelerator, and the Bronco began to move slowly forward.

Dejectedly he had called, "Remember I love you, Kelly."

And she had finally driven away and left him staring after her, cursing herself for not having realized before just how serious things had become from his point of view.

When she reached the clinic, she was relieved there were no more emergency calls to be taken care of but cringed at the six messages from Neil that had come in at various times during the night. Well, she'd have to deal with him later but not now, not when she was bone-weary and having great difficulty staying awake. And what was there to talk about, anyway? She'd never really thought about whether she cared enough for Neil to marry him. Neither did she know if what she did feel could grow into something more. Besides, there was still that niggling little feeling that something, somewhere, was missing.

Since it was early and the Sunday kennel attendant had not yet arrived, she made the rounds to check on hospitalized animals without assistance. The two puppies suffering from *parvo* were holding their own, and the cat that had been chewed up in a dog fight hissed and glared at her with accusing eyes, so she didn't take him out of the cage, figuring if he had that much anger, he was on the road to recovery, anyway.

She up-dated medication charts, and by the time she'd finished, the attendant was there. She gave explicit orders that unless the emergency was a *serious* emergency, he wasn't to call her before four that afternoon, explaining she'd been up all night.

At last, she headed for home. If she didn't feel so *grungy*, she'd just fall on the sofa in her garage apartment without even taking a shower, but delivering twin colts had not left her in the best of hygiene. It was not yet nine, and if she was very quiet, she could ease the Bronco into the drive without her parents' hearing. Her mother would want to know why she wasn't with Neil, because she hadn't told her she was on call. That would have resulted in the usual nagging that Kelly should not let a little thing like her *job* interfere with her romance with Dodie Brandon's wonderful son.

All seemed quiet as she turned into the tree-shaded drive. So far so good. She eased into the garage, quietly got out, and turned to the stairs that would take her to her apartment. She was almost home-free when she cringed at the sound of her mother screeching hysterically from the back door.

"Kelly! Kelly Jean Sanders, you get yourself in here right now! You've got some explaining to do, young lady!"

Kelly wished she could crawl in a hole and pull it in after her. Neil had wasted no time! Wearily, she called, "It will have to wait. I've been up all night, and I'm dead on my feet!"

"No! *Now!*" Verna Sanders struck at the air with

her fists. "I mean it, Kelly Jean. You've gone too far this time!"

She knew she'd never get any peace till her mother had her say. With yet another sigh that made her feel like a slow-leaking tire, she headed for the house.

"In here." Verna waved her frantically inside.

Kelly stepped into the kitchen.

"On in here."

She followed her into the dining room, and that's when she saw it all—the miniature wedding cake centered in the middle of the lace-covered dining room table, flanked with arrangements of fresh flowers. There were silver bowls filled with pastel mints and peanuts. The punch bowl was still empty but ready, no doubt, for champagne.

Kelly's shocked eyes took in the scene, and she groaned. "I don't believe this!"

Verna began to pace around the table. "Neither do I! How could you do this to me? To your family? To Neil? I want you to know he's out of his mind. He's never been so humiliated and embarrassed and neither have I. I've got to call and make excuses to the family, and they were all looking forward to coming over to celebrate your engagement, and—"

"Mother, hold it!" Kelly sharply cried. Things were getting out of hand. "Now you have to hear *my* side. Neil and I never even discussed getting married, and—"

"But he's *perfect* for you!" Verna wailed, waving her arms wildly. "Can't you see that? He's *the* perfect husband. He's rich! He's handsome. He comes from a good family. What more do you want?"

"Love," Kelly said quietly, simply. "The most important quality in a relationship, Mother."

Verna looked at her like she'd lost her mind and cried, "Oh, what do you know about love? You married that god-awful hippie, and we all know how *that* turned out!''

''I made one mistake. I don't intend to make another.''

At that, Verna blazed, ''You will if you let Neil Brandon get away.''

Kelly looked from her mother's angrily contorted face as her father walked into the room. Never had she seen him look quite so miserable. Quietly, he directed himself to Verna, warning, ''If you don't calm down, you're going to have one of your attacks.''

As if on cue and reminded of her favorite weapon, Verna began to cough and wheeze. Clutching the back of a chair, she began to sob, ''I wish God would tell me how I failed as a mother! I did everything in my power to raise that child with morals and values, and she's fought me every step of the way. And now she's going to ruin her life completely and kill me in the process.''

Walter Sanders went to stand by his wife, patting her shoulder in comfort. Staring at Kelly accusingly, he said, ''You've got to get hold of yourself, Verna. Kelly hasn't said she's not going to marry Neil. According to what he told us last night, she was just surprised, and they're going to talk it over and work everything out—''

''But what am I going to tell everyone? If I tell them she can't make up her mind about a wonderful boy like Neil, they'll think there's something wrong with her, and with *me* for raising such a stupid child!''

''Just tell them Neil didn't have a chance to propose last night, that Kelly was on call at the clinic, and he had to postpone his surprise. You can put the cake in the freezer. You don't have to tell them anything else.''

''Oh, yes, she does.''

They looked at Kelly.

Damnit, she couldn't stand the way they were talking as though she wasn't even there, so concerned about making excuses to family and friends. No one cared about *her* feelings. Frostily, furiously, she declared, "You can tell them the truth—that all of you were conniving to put me on the spot so I'd have to agree to marry Neil, and I refused. You can tell them that it was all Neil's doing, and yours, Mother, and Dodie's. I never, not once in my relationship the past six months with Neil, have given him any cause to think I was even *remotely* ready to get engaged. I don't want you making up excuses, stalling. I want you to tell the truth."

Verna coughed, wheezed, clutched the front of her husband's shirt as she struggled to speak. "I . . . I can't do that."

"Yes, you can. It's the only way out of this mess." Kelly turned to go, then paused to add, "And I think you should all know that at the present time, I have no intentions of marrying Neil. I will think about it, maybe in the far distant future, once I get over being mad with him and everybody else behind this scheme, but I think you'd be wise to go ahead and eat that damned cake before it turns to stone in the freezer."

At that, Verna gave a squeaky gasp and collapsed in Walter's arms.

Struggling to lower her to the floor, he shouted at Kelly, "See what you've done? She's having one of her attacks, and it looks like a bad one. Call the paramedics!"

Kelly hurried to the phone, not because she thought her mother was in any real danger but because it was the easiest way out of the difficult situation for the moment. She made the call, then helped her father carry her into the living room and lay her on the sofa. He began to fan her with part of the Sunday paper, as though that would help her breathing, and Kelly took her pulse. It was fast but not alarmingly so. She was convinced she was faking.

Just as the sounds of sirens could be heard in the distance, Kelly heard a car door slam. Seconds later, Neil was bounding through the front door, face ashen, eyes bulging. He stared from Verna lying on the sofa, apparently unconscious, to Kelly and cried, "What's going on? What happened?"

Brusquely, Kelly told him, "Mother had one of her attacks because we didn't get engaged last night."

"Oh, no." He slapped his forehead with the palm of his hand. "Is she going to be all right?"

Walter snapped, "God, I hope so. I just don't know how long she can keep coming out of these things. They get worse every time she has one." He glared at Kelly again. "I thought this time things would be different, that you really wanted this family back together, but I guess I was wrong—*again*. Maybe your coming home was just a big mistake for everybody!"

Kelly bit down on her lip, told herself it was best to just keep her mouth shut because nothing she said then was going to help the ridiculously unbelievable situation.

She watched in silence as the paramedics rushed in with a stretcher and loaded her mother into the ambulance. Her father got in to ride with her. Neighbors were curiously gathering on the lawn, whispering among themselves, wondering what was going on.

"I'll drive you to the hospital," Neil said as they stood on the porch staring at the ambulance driving away.

Kelly shook her head "No, you won't. I'm not going."

She started back inside, but he caught her arm to ask, astonished, "What do you mean? Of course, you are. We both are."

"No, I'm not," she coldly repeated. "I've been up all night, Neil. I'm beat. Besides, I've seen her have these so-called attacks before, and believe me, she's not in any danger. When they get her to the hospital, they'll give her inhalation therapy and then a few tranquilizers. She'll have a nice private room where she can enjoy all the cards and flowers and visits from her friends for the next few days, then she'll come home to start in on me again. Right now, I'm going to bed. Now good-bye. I'll talk to you later."

She closed the door in his astonished face.

After she'd had a shower, she put on her favorite one-size T-shirt, emblazoned with the picture of a very disgruntled cat that had fallen in a toilet bowl and imprinted, *"Don't tell me what kind of day to have!"* It suited her mood.

She made cheese toast, poured herself a glass of milk, then propped up in bed to unwind and try to sort out all the misery. Her father was right. It had been a mistake for her to come home. A *big* mistake. There had been other job offers from other places in the country. Now she knew she should've taken one of them.

On an impulse, she got out of bed and went to her desk where she tossed all of her mail till there was time to go through it. She remembered seeing a monthly newsletter from the veterinary association, found it, and quickly scanned the section on positions currently available. The one soliciting for a vet in Abilene, Texas, leaped out at her. *Large animal practice.* She loved all phases of vet medicine but working with large animals, especially horses, was her first love.

The idea took hold. She had to get away! Escape! Run!

She placed a call to Texas, disappointed to have to leave her name and number with an answering machine. That meant it would be Monday before anyone got back to her. Okay, she would wait. She had to think about giving notice at the clinic, anyway. But what to do till then? She couldn't stand the thoughts of having to listen to her parents' nagging and Neil's cajoling and wheedling.

She tensed at the shrill ringing of the phone. She'd left her answering machine on, thank goodness, but felt like beating her head against the wall at the sound of Neil's pleading voice. "Kelly, honey, are you there? Pick up, please. I know you're tired, but we've got to talk. I've got to tell you how sorry I am that I went about it the wrong way, but it's just because I love you so much, and I want to marry you. I'm at the hospital now, and if you'd just come on over here, it'd make your mother feel better, I know, and—" There was a click. His time was up.

Thank God, she'd set the machine for a short message, or he'd probably have gone on till the tape ran out.

It rang again. She moaned, ran to the bed to burrow her head under the pillow as she heard her father's angry voice demand, "Kelly Jean? Why aren't you here at the hospital? Your mother is asking for you. Now you get yourself over here as fast as you can, and I mean it! And if you aren't here in a half hour, I'm coming after you." He hung up.

Kelly knew she'd had it. Taking out a large tote bag, she crammed in a few clothes, her toiletries, then quickly dressed in jeans and a blouse. No way was she going to stay there and endure this madness. She would check into a motel, near the clinic, and there she'd stay till something came through from Texas—or anywhere! She didn't care at this point where she went, just so she escaped the circus her life seemed to be turning into.

Ready to go, she was about to call the clinic to tell

them she'd phone in later, when she knew where she'd be, when there was an insistent knocking at her door. She froze. *Let them think she was asleep. Maybe they'd give up and go away.*

The knocking became louder, insistent, and then she heard her grandmother Edie's irate voice calling, "You open this door, Kelly! I know you're in there!"

Kelly rushed to let her in. If anyone in the whole world would understand, it was Edie.

Edie never walked into a room—she breezed, like gossamer. And she didn't look anywhere near her age. With her tinted strawberry blonde hair, immaculate makeup, sculptured nails, fashions straight from *Vogue* and a trim figure to show them off to their best advantage, she was a very attractive woman.

She was wearing a pink sweater, matching slacks, and white leather high-heeled boots. Her permed hair hung in ringlets to her shoulders, and she was still hiding the slight bruises from her most recent face lift beneath owl-sized sunglasses. She took one quick look at Kelly's tote bag sitting just inside the door and brusquely demanded, "Where the hell do you think you're going?"

Kelly hung up the phone. She could call later. She flopped on the bed once more and miserably countered, "I can't believe you haven't heard what happened."

"Of course, I did." Edie dropped to the sofa. "I know everything that goes on around here, and it drives your mother mad. But you haven't answered my question. Where do you think you're going?"

"If you know what happened, then you know I've got to get away. I'm going to check into a motel for awhile, and then I'm applying for a job in another state."

Edie's eyebrows shot up. "You mean you're going to just run off, half-cocked, like somebody crazy, all because that boy asked you to marry him?'' She swung her head slowly from side to side in disgust.

Kelly spread her hands in a plea for understanding. ''Edie, you know how Mother is—''

''Do I ever!'' She gave an unladylike snort, rolled her eyes.

''Then surely you can understand why I just want to get away for awhile. She's got her mind made up that I'm going to marry Neil, and he's backing me up against a wall, too. I've bent over backwards trying to make peace with this family, but I'm not going to be pushed into a marriage I don't want. And rather stay and fight about it, I think it'd be best if I just left.'' Her voice rose hysterically, and she swallowed hard, took a deep breath, told herself to calm down.

Edie stared at her thoughtfully for a moment, then quietly asked, ''Don't you think you're being impulsive—*again?''*

Kelly blinked. ''What's that supposed to mean?''

''Need I remind you of the way you just went ahead and dropped out of pre-med before talking it over with your parents? Then when they had a fit, you ran away to England—instead of facing up to them and telling them you just didn't want to be a doctor? And I'd rather not talk about Len!''

''No, please, don't!'' Kelly waved in protest, then challenged, ''So what else is there for me to do? I stay here, and the pressure is on. Mother won't give up, and you know it.''

Edie inspected her nails. Maybe the shade was too pink, but she liked it just the same. Pink made her feel young and romantic.

''Well?'' Kelly prodded. She adored her grandmother, valued her opinion above anyone else's but was determined to escape the madness whether Edie approved or not. ''What would *you* suggest I do?''

Suddenly, Edie smiled. The night before, she'd stayed up late and watched a rerun of that wonderful series, "Love Boat." She had been wanting to go on a cruise for ages but didn't want to go alone. Her friends were either babysitting their grandchildren or too square to be adventureous. Kelly would make the perfect traveling companion, and it was an ideal way for her to get away and re-energize, re-evaluate her life. With an impish grin, she pointed to Kelly's tote bag. "Well, first of all, you need a larger bag."

Kelly blinked, confused. "What are you talking about?"

Edie got up, moved to stand by the door, jingling the keys to her 300Z. "You'll need some new clothes, too. Cocktail dresses, party clothes. The mall is open today. And forget checking into a motel. You're moving in with me till I can make all the arrangements. Verna will have a fit, but that's what she does best, anyway."

Kelly was totally baffled. "What are you talking about. Arrangements for *what?*"

"We're going to *let ourselves go*, as they say."

Kelly could only stare at her, bewildered.

Edie walked over to give her a big hug, then happily announced, "We're going on a cruise!"

"I can't afford a cruise, and don't tell me you'll pay for it. I still owe you for sending me through vet school, and don't say it's just early inheritance. I intend to pay you back every cent!"

"So?" Edie cocked her head to one side and grinned. "Add the cruise to the tab. I need a traveling companion. You'll be doing both of us a favor."

Kelly started to protest once more, but then, slowly, realization took hold that perhaps Edie had hit on a great idea. Finally, she laughed and said, "You know,

Grandma, you might just have yourself a traveling companion!''

Edie made a face. ''You know I hate it when you call me *grandma*, Kelly *Jean*.''

A play of a smile touched Kelly's lips. She knew it only too well and reminded, ''And I hate it when you call me Kelly Jean.''

Edie gave her a playful slap on her bottom and cried, ''Deal! Now let's get going. *Edie* and *Kelly* are going on a cruise and *Edie* just might buy herself a bikini!''

THREE

Edie had chosen a small ship for several reasons. The *Star Princess* only carried around two hundred passengers, but each cabin was outside and offered a magnificent view. Also, even though full amenities and similar facilities of larger cruise ships were offered, she felt the smaller size reminded more of a private yacht.

She and Kelly were going to have absolute freedom to do anything they wanted, when they wanted, or just do nothing at all. And that was the theme of life she wanted them both to experience for the next two weeks. Entertainment was low-key, and the activity schedule light. Onboard life would be refreshingly devoid of the tired old fun and games that routinely appeared on most other ships. She wanted Kelly to enjoy herself, of course, but felt she also vitally needed some quality *alone* time to re-evaluate her life and goals.

Edie stood at the bow of the ship, enjoying the view of Fort Lauderdale on port side, the glistening blue of the Atlantic ocean on starboard. As she sipped the complimentary champagne that waiters in white jackets eagerly provided as they waited to sail, she couldn't help gloating a bit over the way she'd more or less kidnapped Kelly. They'd had a mad, whirlwind shopping excursion that afternoon when the idea had struck. Even though Kelly was exhausted, the excitement gave her the energy to get through the rest of the day. And, fortunately, there'd been no more emergency calls from the clinic.

Edie thought of other times, other ships. In the last five years of Richard's life, when they'd dared to hope the cancer had been defeated, they had taken a cruise every winter. Now, three years since his death, this was the first time she'd been on a ship without him.

Theirs had not been a storybook marriage; there'd been many stormy times. The only thing they constantly agreed on was that their only son had married a neurotic, social climber, who led him around by his nose. Richard had also felt that Verna was wrong to try and dictate Kelly's life. So he'd have been behind her one hundred percent now to aid Kelly in getting herself together.

Edie felt great satisfaction in remembering how she'd been able to so quickly put the rest of her plan in motion. After their shopping spree, Kelly had gone to bed at her apartment, falling asleep at once. Then Edie got on the phone, grateful she knew so many people in Charlotte, thanks to Richard's thriving real estate business. First, she had called Tom Zealey, a close friend, who owned the North Side Animal Hospital where Kelly worked. There had never been a need for Kelly to know *she* held the lease on the building, and that Tom had easily been persuaded to hire Kelly at her prompting. All Edie had to do was ask if he'd mind if Kelly went with her on a much-needed cruise, and he'd not objected. Next, she had called her travel agent, Sudie Cameron, at home, to ask her to arrange a cruise first thing Monday morning, emphasizing departure as soon as possible. Asked for her preferences as to ships, Edie had chosen the *Star Princess*. Sudie had gone to work on it first thing, and by the time Kelly woke up to coffee and croissants in bed around ten they were booked to leave Thursday out of Fort Lauderdale.

"So fast?" Kelly had sleepily questioned. "But my job! I can't just walk off without any warning. And Mother is in the hospital, and—"

"Nonsense!" Edie had waved away her protests, then confided she'd taken care of things at the clinic and reminded they both knew Verna's attacks were exaggerated, if not entirely faked. Cynically, she had warned, "I'll bet if she finds out our plans, she'll check herself out of the hospital and be waiting on the pier at Fort Lauderdale to try and stop us. That's why we're getting out of here this afternoon on a three o'clock flight. We'll just stay at a nice oceanfront hotel and get started on our tan."

Kelly could not resist goading, "And *you're* the one who accused *me* of being impulsive!"

Edie had been quick to justify. "It's only impulsive when you do something without thinking about it first. I've thought about every detail."

"It's still running away," Kelly had teased.

"But you aren't alone. I'm with you."

Kelly had continued to playfully provoke, "But don't you think I need to be alone?"

"Nope!" Edie had disagreed. "Just *left* alone. There's a difference."

"Now you sound like Greta Garbo!" Kelly had laughed.

Edie had laughed along with her. "Maybe. But I'm not about to live like a hermit, and neither are you!"

From the airport, Edie had phoned Walter to inform him that she and Kelly were off on a well-needed vacation. He blew sky-high, as she had known he would, and when she at first refused to tell him exactly where they were off to, he had shown unbelievable bravado and threatened that if she didn't tell him, he'd hire a private detective to track them down. Edie doubted he'd go that far and said so, but then he pointed out that Verna was in the hospital, and it was terribly cruel and callous of her to just spirit their daughter away at such a time. Edie decided maybe she was being a bit paranoid. After all, what could they really do to stop them? So she'd said they were taking a Caribbean cruise and let it go at that.

As for Neil, well, Edie figured he was a big boy. Let him stew. She didn't blame Kelly for being so upset over such a cheap trick of attempted manipulation. Thank God, Kelly got her spirit from *her* and didn't take after her jellyfish of a father. There were times Edie was truly convinced there'd been a mix-up in the hospital all those years ago, and that that spineless man could not really be *her* son!

She was wearing a huge, wide-brimmed hat, ever cautious of the sun on her face. Sun, like age, caused wrinkles. Face-lifts helped and so did the hat. Still, it was a royal pain to have to constantly be on guard. She'd have much preferred to be a sun-worshipper.

"There you are!"

She turned to see Kelly hurrying across the deck, looking happy and rejuvenated already.

"This ship is absolutely wonderful!" She exulted, having just completed her own private tour. "There's a complete spa, a sauna, a steam room, and you can even have herbal body wraps. And there's a swimming pool, three outdoor whirlpools, and a casino and two lounges, a veranda cafe indoors and out, even a disco. I'm surprised a smaller ship like this has so much to offer."

Edie had gone to the bow immediately after coming

onboard so had not seen their cabin and asked Kelly what it was like.

"Gorgeous! And *huge!* We've got twin beds, walk-in closets, a refrigerator loaded with wine and mix and Cokes and beer. There's a separate sitting area looking out on the ocean, but we've still got a great view when we're in bed." She threw her arms around Edie and gave her a big hug. "How can I ever thank you? This is just what I need!"

"What we *both* need," Edie pointed out. "I haven't done anything like this since your grandfather died."

"Then this is an escape for both of us."

"Exactly. And when we get home, we'll both have a new perspective on life."

Kelly dared asked, "Does that mean you'll start accepting some of those invitations you're always getting from nice, lonely widowers?"

"You never know." She winked.

At last, they sailed, amidst a lively steel drum playing its own version of "Anchors Aweigh." Then there was the required lifeboat drill. Finally, they went to their cabin, where Edie agreed they did have extremely nice accommodations.

After dinner, where they met so many amiable fellow passengers, they attended a cruise staff show. There was also a brief talk to prepare them for their first port of call early the next morning—Nassau.

"You'll love Nassau," Edie assured Kelly. "Crystal blue water, white sand beaches, plus the best *Yellowbirds* in the Bahamas," she added, referring to the popular rum concoction of the islands.

It was nearly eleven o'clock when they left the cruise show, and neither was ready to end the day. They went on to the disco, and Kelly was delighted that an older gentleman at once asked Edie to slow dance.

There were a few other unattached men onboard, all

much older than Kelly, but she enjoyed their company all the same. After all, she wanted to have fun—not romance. *That* was the last thing on her mind, especially when she was still desperately trying to discover what was missing in her relationship with Neil. Did she really love him but was just afraid to admit it? So many questions waiting to be answered.

When they retired around one A.M., they fell asleep right away, exhausted. The next morning, Kelly bounded out of bed, anxious for her first glimpse of Nassau. Edie, awakened by her stirring, sleepily wanted to know if it was as beautiful as she'd said it was.

Kelly was puzzled, because the ship wasn't moving, but yet they weren't in port. She said as much to Edie, who got up to pad across the floor and look out the window with her.

"Something is wrong," Kelly said, feeling apprehension creeping. "Let's get dressed and go find out what this is all about. We were scheduled to arrive during the night."

Just then, the announcement came over the loudspeaker in the hall outside their door. "Ladies and gentlemen, this is your captain speaking. I regret to inform you that the *Star Princess* has experienced a problem. All passengers are asked to report at once to the Starlight Lounge for further briefing."

They dressed quickly and hurried to the lounge, which was fast filling up with equally alarmed passengers. As soon as everyone was assembled, the captain, himself, appeared to explain that it appeared a propeller shaft was broken. They would be towed into Nassau, but the cruise could not continue. Repairs would take several days.

Everyone groaned and began to murmur among themselves. The cruise director got up to announce that they would all be flown back to Fort Lauderdale as soon as possible, and they would each be given a free cruise on the *Star Princess* at a future date. They were all asked to return to their cabins and pack their belongings, and as soon as they were towed into port, they'd be transferred to the airport.

Kelly and Edie looked at each other in shared frustration. "Well," Kelly said finally, "I guess there's nothing to do but go home and face the music."

Edie's eyebrows shot up. "Are you crazy? We're not going home now, not when I've bought all those new clothes. And your mother is probably out of the hospital by now, sitting there like a spider waiting to leap on both of us. No way! I've got to rest up for *that* encounter. We'll just check into a hotel in Nassau for as long as we like."

Kelly liked that idea, but as soon as they got ashore, they quickly found out that it was "high" season for tourists and all the hotels were booked solid. Some of the other passengers on the *Star Princess* had the same idea and were disgruntled to have no choice but be shuttled on to the airport to return home.

Edie was determined they were not going to do that. Kelly said she'd sent flowers to her mother before they'd left, and a note saying she wished things could be different. Still, she knew it would be like Edie predicted—constant nagging and harping, and she'd probably be driven to run away the very first night and join the Peace Corps or something equally as liberating from her mother's hysterical wrath.

They had hired a cab to drive them around from hotel to hotel. Though it was frustrating to be told again and again there were no vacancies, Kelly was enjoying the beauty of the island. There was a riot of color in the oleanders, hibiscus, poinsettias, and the myriad of other flora. She delighted in the birds everywhere—flamingos, parrots, canaries. There were old wooden or pastel-tinted coral houses with louver windows and balconies overhanging the often walled-in streets—Georgian and Federal style architecture for the most part.

Finally, their driver, a dark-skinned native with a thick accent regretfully told them, "Ladies, I am very sorry, but there is no more. We have been to every hotel on the island."

They were back at the waterfront, teeming with activity as bicycles and fringe-topped surreys vied for space on the narrow street. Inter-island vessels were moving in and out from the piers and farther out boats of all kinds could be seen—motorboats, sailboats, now and then a schooner.

"Maybe we could rent our own yacht," Edie said thoughtfully.

Kelly shook her head and laughed. Her grandmother was absolutely indomitable. "No, I think we've got to admit we're defeated this time. We can always stay in Fort Lauderdale a few days."

"It's not the same as the islands."

Suddenly, their driver snapped his fingers, turned around in his seat to flash a wide grin, brown eyes shining. "Hey! You want islands? I know the perfect one for you. It's small, but they have good accommodations."

"You've convinced us." Kelly went on to qualify, "As long as it's peaceful and quiet, we'll like it."

He drove on down the narrow street beside the waterfront, seemed to be looking for something as he went on to say, "You'll get plenty peace, believe me. Ah, there he is!" He stopped the cab, pointed to a grayhaired man working with the lines to a fishing boat. "That is Captain Burt Grady. He comes from Harbour Island every day around this time to sell his day's catch. He can take you over there."

Edie and Kelly watched as he got out and hurried over

to the pier to talk to the captain. "Are you sure this is what you want to do?" Edie asked anxiously, and Kelly assured it was, pointing out it was an *adventure*, and they'd probably wind up having more fun than they would have on the cruise.

Captain Grady came over to the cab to introduce himself. Kelly guessed he was about the same age as Edie, except that he had lots of wrinkles. Deeply tanned from the sun and sea, his skin was almost like leather, but he had a healthy, happy, glow about him. It was obvious his lifestyle agreed with him.

"I'll be glad to take you over to the island," he affably told them. "It's about a half hour ride, but the sea is pretty calm today. Ought to be a real nice trip."

When their luggage was loaded onto the boat, the cab driver amply rewarded for his time and assistance, they were on their way. Edie, not wanting her hat to blow off or be in the sun, sat up front with the captain under the little roof over the steering compartment.

Kelly opted to sit out on deck, loving the taste of the salt air and the cool breeze ruffling her hair. The boat, she noted, though nice, was far from luxurious. It reeked with the smell of fish and bait, and there were buckets and fishing poles lying about, nets and hooks, and even a few oars for emergencies. There was a big hatch door in the middle, and she assumed that was where Captain Grady stowed his catch till he went to Nassau to sell it.

Never had she seen water so blue, and as they drew closer to Harbour Island, the sea became translucently turquoise, then blended to jade green, purple, aquamarine, mauve, lemon yellow, and even a shade of apricot blending to rose. Kelly was absolutely mesmerized by the beautiful spectacle. Ahead, the beach was a strip of incredibly *pink* sand, fringed beyond by the same rainbow hue of flowers she'd seen in Nassau.

Captain Grady slowed the engines as they drew nearer

to a pier extending out in the water. He turned around to apologize to Kelly for the lack of excitement ashore. "Young folks like you prefer the casinos and nightclubs of Nassau. There's just not much here like that. Oh, we've got good seafood places, and once in awhile, there'll be a cook-out and party right on the beach, but other than that, unless you're in to fishing or diving, you won't find much going on. I go over to Nassau just about every day, so any time you want to hitch a ride with me, you're welcome."

She thanked him, said she was sure she'd have a wonderful time.

When they reached shore, Captain Grady wouldn't let them pay him anything and even insisted on firing up his old pickup truck to drive them to the nicest hotel on the island—the Sea Gull.

"From a 'Z' to a pickup!" Kelly could not resist teasing Edie when they were alone. "Talk about slumming!"

"Hey, I'm having a great time!" Edie was quick to inform. "You're the spoiled brat in the crowd, and you're the one who's going to miss the discos and bars."

"We'll see!" Kelly was already in love with the island and didn't think she was going to miss anything civilization had to offer—not for awhile, anyway.

The hotel was not very large and typical island fare. Two stories only, a wide veranda swept three sides. There was a small parlor and reception area downstairs, with a kitchen, and a small, but adequate, dining room. Upstairs, there were only twelve rooms, six on each side of a narrow hallway.

Their rooms adjoined, and Edie pointed out there was no telephone, radio, or TV in either, and Kelly promptly cried, "Who cares?" as she hugged herself and whirled around the room. "It's paradise!"

"And I'm exhausted!" Edie declared. They were in her room, and she sprawled on the bed and said she was going to take a nap. "Traipsing all over Nassau this afternoon wore me out. Wake me for dinner."

Kelly was not about to go to bed, not when there was so much exploring to be done. Changing from skirt and blouse and sandals into shorts, T-shirt, and sneakers, she tied her hair back in a pony tail, grabbed up her sunglasses and took off. She'd already spotted the "Mopeds For Rent" sign across the street and knew exactly how she wanted to spend the rest of her day.

The island, Kelly soon discovered, was probably about two and a half miles long and about a mile and half square in area. Dunmore Town was the main settlement, old and charming with a protected harbor. She saw signs offering tourists good snorkeling, spear-fishing, and skindiving. The few and only slightly sloping hills above were lush with banana trees and coconut palms, swaying gently in the tropical breeze. Residents seemed friendly, waving and smiling as she passed.

As the sun began to sink into the azure waters in a blaze of peach and crimson glory, she paused to watch the activity at the waterfront. The chartered deep-sea fishing boats chugged into port, and sun-blistered tourists, weary and worn, came ashore.

The salt air and tropical breeze was exhilarating, and Kelly didn't want to go back to the hotel. Edie needed her rest, and *she* wanted time to herself. She decided to explore a bit more. In talking to one of the natives, she'd been told that the south end of the island was most remote. The road there was not paved, sparsely inhabited. That sounded wonderful to her, and she took off in that direction on the perky little Moped.

She delighted in the discovery of a very private cove, rimmed on each side by a slightly inclining rocky bluff. A smooth, pinkish-tinted beach was sandwiched between. It was perfect for swimming, with few swells and no breakers. The water was so clear she could see the bottom.

Hot and sweaty from the island humidity and her ride, Kelly wished she'd brought her bathing suit. Glancing around and noting once more just how isolated it was, she could not resist yielding to temptation.

As she began to undress, a colorful macaw screeched curiously from his perch in a swaying palm tree. Laughing up at him, she called, "What's the matter? Haven't you ever seen anyone swim naked before?"

She waded out in the water, reveling in the coolness. Then she dove forward and down, opening her eyes to marvel at the crystal clear depths. She could see all kinds of shells, and little schools of brightly colored fish darting about.

As a child, she'd been sent to camp each and every summer, where it was hoped she'd learn some discipline and how to conform to society, in general. But, much to her parents' surprise, she hadn't had any problems obeying the rules there, got along well with counselors and fellow campers alike. And she had learned many things—like how to weave baskets and wallets and Indian moccasins, identify poison ivy and oak. Most of all, however, she'd become an expert swimmer.

She swam underwater for awhile, then surfaced to lay back and float along in the late evening glow, marveling at the exhilarating sense of peace that prevailed. This, she decided, would be her private haven during her time at the island, and she thereby christened it "Paradise Cove." Here, the problems back home seemed so very far away. She could push them back into the dark recesses of her mind and refuse to let them surface to needle. And maybe, somewhere along the way, a miracle would happen, and she'd have the magic answer as to how to deal with her parents, Neil, her whole life. But, for the moment, she wanted only to let her mind flow peacefully, freely, as she gave herself up to the gentle water of her secluded inlet.

Suddenly, there was a loud splash, and she was at once frightened, but alert. She dove down, came up to tread water, gasping in terror to see the large dog swimming purposefully towards her. At the same instant, she saw the young man standing on the beach. He was waving his arms and laughing as he called, "Don't panic. He won't hurt you. He just thought you were a big fish."

Big, fish, indeed! Kelly fumed as the large, mixed-breed dog approached, eyes friendly, tail wagging like a rudder. What she wanted to know was how long the mutt's owner had been spying on her as she lazily floated along, spread-eagled and naked! And how was she supposed to get out of the water when her clothes were back there, on the beach?

The dog, satisfied she wasn't edible, fell in beside her to swim towards shore. When her toes could touch bottom, Kelly remained in the water up to her shoulders and called to the staring stranger, "Would you mind going away so I can come out? As you probably noticed, I'm not wearing a bathing suit."

"I couldn't help but notice," he yelled back, grinning. "Nice view but a little distant."

Kelly wasn't really angry. After all, what guy wouldn't look at a girl floating naked? But the fun was over, and it was time he left so she could get dressed. She also had to admit a bit of apprehension at her somewhat vulnerable situation. The cove *was* isolated, and he could be some kind of a pervert, though he didn't look the part. At that distance, even though he was wearing sunglasses, she could tell he was quite good-looking with sun-bleached hair, tall, well built, tanned to a golden bronze. His chest was broad, with a mat of also bleached hair trailing downwards to disappear into his bikini-style swimsuit. She could not resist noticing he was well-developed in *that* department, too. Still, she felt uneasy, indignantly demanded, "Will you *please* get out of here, so I can get dressed? What are you? A weirdo-pervert who hangs around private beaches hoping to see a little skin?"

At that, his smile faded. "This happens to be *my* beach, lady. I live here. Through those trees back there." He hooked his thumb over his shoulder indicating a gently rising slope.

Kelly squinted against the evening sun. She couldn't see anything. But, if he lived here, he was no threat, and it probably was his beach. Now she felt foolish.

Abruptly turning on his heel, he started to walk away, yelling over his shoulder, "Go on and get out. I won't look." He couldn't resist adding to goad her, "I've probably seen better, anyway."

She paddled ashore quickly, pulled on her clothes. Then, feeling a bit devilish, yielded to temptation and fired back, "Bet you haven't, either!"

He turned, just as she struck a provocative pose.

"Sorry," he laughed, "I still need a closer look to judge."

She got on her Moped, started the little motor. "Well, that's all you're gonna get, mister!" She gave a salute of her own and left the beach in a roar and spray of sand.

Yet, as she headed back into town and the Sea Gull hotel, Kelly could not help smiling to herself. He *was* cute, and when he'd looked at her that last time, he had pushed his sunglasses up on his forehead, and even from a distance she could tell he had nice eyes—crinkled at the corners from the sun, a bright azure color, like the sea.

Maybe, she thought mischievously, she'd swim in the cove again tomorrow. He could judge what she looked like in a bikini. She already liked what *she* had seen of *his*.

There was, she told herself, no harm in a little flirting, a little fun. She could just pretend this was *Fantasy Island*, and she was going to escape the real world, if only for a little while—and made up her mind then and there to enjoy every single minute.

FOUR

Edie and Kelly enjoyed a breakfast in the Sea Gull's small, but adequate, dining room. They sat by an open window, drinking in the sweet morning air and marveling at the view of shimmering sky-hued water in the distance. They were served fried bananas, sprinkled with cinnamon and powdered sugar, along with steaming coffee, thick and rich, and glasses of freshly squeezed limeade.

Afterwards, Edie announced, "Now I'm going to take a book I brought along and stake out one of those rocking chairs on the front porch for the rest of the day."

Reluctantly, Kelly said she thought she'd better call home. "If Mom and Dad hear the cruise was cancelled, they'll get worried if they don't hear from us."

"So, let them stew," Edie said airily. "They're happiest when they've got something to worry about. Besides," she pointed out, eyes narrowed accusingly, "you were going to run away and hide, anyway, remember? So why are you feeling guilty now?"

"I'd just feel better if I called. Besides, if I do, Mom

won't be able to say she didn't know how to get in touch with us in an emergency, so that will give her one less thing to gripe about when we do get back.''

"Well, you go right ahead. I've lived this long without answering to your mother for *my* whereabouts, and I'm not starting now."

Kelly had spotted a telephone depot the day before, where she could call the states with a credit card. After first stopping to rent another Moped for the day, she then went to place her call.

As she had expected, her mother began an angry tirade the instant she recognized her voice. "Kelly Jean, where are you? How dare you just take off like that, with me sick in the hospital? I was just discharged yesterday. Heavens, they were talking about putting me in ICU, and I kept telling them it was just nerves, because my only child is breaking my heart. I swear, you're going to be the death of me, yet! And you can tell your grandmother I'll never forgive her for her part in this. And don't try to tell me she wasn't behind it all. She's undermined me your whole life, criticizing me behind my back, making you resentful and rebellious, and—"

"Mother, listen to me!" Kelly interrupted loudly, sternly. "I didn't call to argue. I just wanted to let you know the cruise was cancelled in Nassau because the ship had problems. But we're staying on one of the islands for awhile, and—"

"The cruise was canceled?" Verna screeched in echo. "And you're staying on one of the islands?"

"Yes, we're on a place called Harbour Island. We couldn't find a room in Nassau. Everything was booked. I just wanted to let you know we're okay and see how you're doing."

"How do you *think* I'm doing? And why are you even bothering to ask, when you obviously don't care?

You never think of anybody but yourself. You've always been like that. And dear God, to think I nearly died giving birth to you, and this is the way you repay me! You ran off while I was still in the hospital, didn't even come to see me! I'm embarrassed and humiliated in front of my friends.

"You get yourself home as fast as you can, Kelly Jean," she continued her tirade after pausing just long enough to take a breath, "and I mean it. You've got a job, and you've also got a fiance who's worried sick about you. And your wild behavior is going to put me in an early grave, and—" She began to wheeze and cough, threatening another attack.

"I am not coming home just yet," Kelly said quickly, firmly, "and I *don't* have a *fiance*. I'm going to hang up now, because you're just getting upset. Tell Dad hello. I'll send you a postcard. Don't worry about us. Now, good-bye."

"Kelly Jean, don't you dare hang up on me—"

Kelly replaced the receiver, stepped out of the booth. She took a deep breath, let it out slowly, attempting to expel some of the rage and frustration. Edie had been right. It *had* been a mistake to call. Still, her conscience was clear now, and at least she couldn't be accused of not letting her family know where they were.

She went down to the main pier to watch the boats for awhile. Then, tiring of that, decided to go for another exploring ride on the Moped. Just as she was about to take off, she heard the sound of an animal whimpering, as though in pain. It seemed to be coming from beneath the pier, so she went around to look and saw the same scruffy dog that had mistaken her for dinner the night before. He was licking his paw and whining. "Hey, boy," she called gently, "come here and let me see what's wrong with that foot."

He stopped licking and looked at her with curious

but hopeful eyes. Kelly was well aware, even without her veterinary training, that it could be extremely dangerous to approach a strange dog that was injured. She held out her hand to let him sniff it, to sense she meant him no harm. He did so, then wagged his tail but made no move to come to her. With a sigh of resignation, she knew there was nothing to do but crawl beneath that pier with the crabs and water spiders.

Giving his paw a cursory examination, it appeared he had stepped on a piece of glass. It needed to come out. "Stay here," she commanded, even though he didn't look like he was going anywhere. Crawling out, she hurried to a general store across the street from the waterfront. There, she bought peroxide, a needle, and a pair of tweezers. The dog was waiting, and as she worked as gently as possible to extract the sliver of glass, he didn't move or make a sound. Finally, she had it, then rinsed out the wound with peroxide. With a pat on his head, she declared, "I think you'll be good as new now, fella."

He followed her, wagging his tail happily. Having found a new friend, he didn't want to lose her. "Hey, you can't go with me," she told him. "I'm going for a ride, and it's dangerous for you to run alongside. Besides, you need to rest that paw so it will stop bleeding."

"Hey, you've got my dog!" A male voice called from out on the pier.

Kelly looked up to see the stranger she'd encountered in the cove the previous evening. He was walking away from an impressive boat he'd just tied up, a trawler she guessed to be about forty feet in length.

He jumped down to stand beside her on the beach, leaning to ruffle the dog's hair. "Hey, Biscuit, I've been looking all over for you, boy. Is this pretty girl trying to kidnap you?"

Kelly's eyebrows shot up. "What did you call him? *Biscuit?*"

"Yeah, that's the only way to get him to come to you—make him think he's going to get food. Isn't that right, boy?" He patted him again, then saw he was holding up his paw for inspection. He knelt to look at it, as Kelly explained about the glass.

She handed him the bottle of peroxide. "It will be okay. Just rinse it out with this a few times today and again tomorrow, and I don't think it will get infected. If it starts swelling or turns pink, or if he won't quit licking it, you might want to check with your local vet."

"We don't have one on the island." He straightened, appraising her with his eyes and liking what he saw. He held out his hand. "That was real nice of you. Thanks. I'm Mike Kramer, by the way."

"And I'm Kelly Sanders . . . *by the way*," she smiled. Standing close, she knew she'd been right the day before in thinking he had nice eyes—and they *were* blue. "We met yesterday, *sort of*," she couldn't resist impishly adding.

"Oh, I remember that, all right," he laughed softly, then took on a sober note. "I guess I should apologize. I probably embarrassed you."

"I wasn't embarrassed. Just leery of having a guy spy on me that way."

"Hey, I wasn't spying," he was quick to correct, though not indignantly. "I was about to go swimming myself, and, like I said, that's *my* beach."

"Sorry. I didn't know. I won't do it again."

"You're welcome any time, especially since you took care of Biscuit. I was wondering why he wasn't around this morning when I left in the boat. I guess he was nursing his wound.

"By the way," he went on, still taking her in with

his eyes. "What brings you to Harbour Island? Your age group usually stays in Nassau, where the discos and casinos are. There's nothing here but lonely beaches and perverts lurking behind the palm trees hoping to catch a glimpse of *skin*," he added with a wink.

Kelly liked his easy-going way. She told him about the aborted cruise and not being able to find a vacancy in Nassau, how Captain Grady brought her and Edie over and sent them to the Sea Gull.

"Captain Grady is a fine man," Mike assured, "and it's a shame your vacation turned out like it did, but if you're looking for peace and quiet, you'll find it here."

"What do *you* find here?" She suddenly found the need to know. "I mean, you talk about *my* age group. Aren't *you* included in that, too? So where do you go for fun?"

They had walked over to a shady spot beneath the gently clattering leaves of a grove of banana trees. There was a bench, and they sat down, with Biscuit promptly crawling underneath to lie down and nurse his wound.

Mike told her he found plenty to do when he wanted to make the bar scene, but mostly his business kept him busy. Pointing to a small, squat building sitting right on the water next to the pier where they'd met, he told her, "That's my dive shop. I sell and rent equipment, and I specialize in scuba diving excursions for tourists who want to go below to see the coral reefs, spear-fish, and so on. If you're into diving, there's always something to do. There's a shipwreck that's always interesting to see, and I even know of an underwater cave where I sometimes take people for a special kind of picnic."

"Picnic?" Kelly echoed. *"Underwater?"*

"Sure. It's beautiful there. I discovered it myself." He went on to explain how food and other supplies were sealed in plastic bags, but as he talked, he was thinking how it wasn't only her looks that he found so appealing. He was used to being around pretty girls who were drop-dead sexy in skimpy bikinis, even though he had to admit the sight of her floating naked was a scene he'd never forget. There was something else about her that he'd liked at once—spirit. Kelly Sanders exuded spirit and spunk and a zest for life. Yet, within the lovely depths of those brooding hazel eyes, he sensed some anxiety, just as he could tell she was uptight, not at all in tune with the easy pace of the islands. Perhaps that would come later. He knew only in that moment that he wanted to get to know her better.

"I've always wanted to learn how to dive," Kelly admitted. "Is it difficult?"

"Not really. I give diving lessons, too."

"I'm a good swimmer." Feeling a bit embarrassed, afraid it might sound like she was bragging, she told him about the ribbons she'd won in summer camp competition.

He explained how it wasn't necessary to be an expert swimmer in order to take up diving. "You just have to feel at ease in the water. It gives you self-confidence and self-reliance in case you ever have equipment failure. The main requirement is to have certain physical, mental, and physiological qualifications to understand the principals involved in diving."

"What else?" She was eager to know. The thought of learning to dive was exciting, and she had to admit the thought of Mike Kramer teaching her was also enticing.

"Well, first of all, I'd introduce you to the basics of snorkeling. That way you'd learn how to use a mask, snorkel, and fins. We'd do that in my cove, and—"

"*Paradise Cove,*" she corrected coquettishly, confiding, "I gave it a name already. Hope you don't mind."

He pretended astonishment, snapped his fingers. "Hey, would you believe that's the name *I* gave it when I came here five years ago?"

She shook her head, the play of a smile on her lips.

"I didn't think so," he shook his head in unison, then stood. "Come on. I'll treat you to lunch for taking care of Biscuit, and then we can go over to my shop, and I'll show you around. I didn't have anything scheduled today, so I haven't opened yet. I'll give you a complete rundown on what's involved in learning to dive, and you can make up your mind whether or not you want to go for it."

She took the hand he held out to her because it seemed so natural, and she reveled in the way his fingers gently caressed. It was like a secret message that meant he liked her, a lot, and she squeezed back, transcending one of her own. Good grief, she told her pounding heart, what madness was this? One day on a Caribbean island and a sun-tanned hunk was making her heart pound like never before. *Enjoy!* Her brain commanded. *Let yourself go. That's why you're here! The misery you left behind will still be there waiting for you when you get back. Make the most of this day and fret about tomorrow when it gets here.*

He took her to the Mariner, a cafe she hadn't noticed earlier because it was situated at the end of a narrow, cobblestone alley. Pots of flowering hibiscus were just outside the red-painted door which was set in a stone wall at least eight feet high. Biscuit, who'd limped along behind them, settled down once more in the shade to patiently wait.

Inside, Kelly was delighted to find it was actually a courtyard, abundant with hanging baskets filled with flowers and greenery. There was a tall bubbling fountain in the middle, surrounded by thick banana and palm trees, with colorful parrots sitting freely amidst the foliage. Small tables, seating no more than four chairs each, were positioned about the room. An umbrella-like net was draped above and adorned with huge palm fronds for shelter from the blistering sun. There was a tiny roof at the very fringes of the court-yard, for those who didn't want such open dining, and also for refuge when it rained.

"It's lovely," Kelly said at once. "I had no idea this existed. In fact, the more I learn about Harbour Island, the more convinced I am that it's a well-guarded secret."

"Well, don't tell anybody," he said with mock con-cern. "We don't want word to get out. We like it fine, just the way it is."

"More tourists, more dollars."

"Some people value solitude more."

"Right. And I'm one of them. I won't tell a soul. But what about your diving business? It would increase if there was more traffic."

He explained that really wasn't a problem. "In fact, I find I have to turn excursions down once in a while." He went on to tell how he was registered with several of the big hotels in Nassau, and their tourist agents booked groups for him.

A pretty dark-skinned girl in a white uniform came out of an archway from the kitchen and greeted Mike effusively. "Where have you been? Working too hard, again! You know you need my good cooking to keep you healthy." Rolling inquisitive dark eyes in Kelly's direction, she flashed a knowing grin. "You have a special guest, yes?"

He introduced Kelly, then said, "Kelly, meet Anna. Her father owns this place, but Anna does all the cooking."

"Anna does *all the work!*" Anna brusquely, cheerily added.

Kelly liked her at once.

As Mike led the way to a table near the fountain, Anna wanted to know if she'd like to take a chance on native food and try the day's special. "Sure. I'm always ready to experiment. Keeps life interesting."

Mike ordered yellowbirds for them, and Kelly took one sip and pronounced the sweet and spicy tropical drink delicious. They were having their second when Anna brought out a platter that she explained was grilled quail with mango-papaya sauce.

"How do you stay so skinny?" Kelly asked Mike after only one bite of the luscious cuisine. "If I'm not careful, between the drinks and the food, I'll weigh a ton before I go home."

"Not with all the swimming we're going to be doing," Mike reminded, "that is, if you're serious about wanting to learn how to dive."

"Of course, I am. For the time I'm here, I want to try everything."

"And how long will that be?" he wanted to know, trying not to appear anxious. As much as he liked her already, past experience told him not to get his hopes up that they might truly hit it off. She might be like so many of the others—out for a summer romance and nothing more. Since the last time he'd been burned, he'd more or less made that his credo, too, but there was just something about Kelly Sanders that warned he'd better be on guard lest his heart want something more than just a fling.

Kelly was thoughtful for a moment. The cruise was to have lasted two weeks. She supposed they'd have to go back at the end of that time and try to deal with the situation with her parents and Neil. Finally, she said,

"I'm really not sure. A couple of weeks, anyway. Is that long enough?"

"Sure, if you catch on fast and do as I say. It isn't that hard. The most important thing is to learn how to use and adjust your equipment. We'll get you started on snorkeling tomorrow. After lunch, I'll show you what we'll be using, go over it with you at my shop. That is . . ." he let his voice trail as he reached to squeeze her hand across the table, then finished, "if you don't have other plans."

"No, I don't." Dear Lord, why did she tremble at his touch? She drew her fingers back self-consciously, lifted her drink to take a sip before explaining, "But first I should go back and check on Edie. She'll probably be wondering where I disappeared to."

"I'll go with you, if you don't mind. I'd like to meet her."

"I'm sure she'd like to meet you, too." She was confident Edie would take to him right away. He seemed so happy, so full of life—the kind of people she enjoyed being around.

Over dessert, a butterscotch and lime pie topped with thick, rich cream, Mike began to delicately question Kelly about herself. He asked where her home was, what she did there. She told him, and he was impressed with her profession. "A lady vet. That explains why you were so good with Biscuit."

"Taking out a sliver of glass doesn't exactly require a degree in veterinary medicine," she pointed out with a laugh.

"Maybe so, but Biscuit doesn't take to strangers. He must've sensed you knew what you were doing." He went on to lament, "I wish we had a vet on the island, but we don't. Not enough dogs or cats around, I suppose, to support one. I take Biscuit to the clinic in

Nassau when he needs anything. Unfortunately, most people can't afford to do that.''

Kelly was reminded of her mother's criticism of how she donated her time to the animal shelter back home, treating stray dogs and cats without charge in order to get them healthy enough to be adopted into good homes. It was something she really enjoyed doing because it gave her a good feeling.

Outside, in the warm sunshine, Mike showed her points of local interest as they walked towards her hotel. Many things went unnoticed behind the stone walls lining the main street: a dental and medical clinic, a modest-size library. There was another street she'd not seen the day before, with several gift shops, a couple of clothing stores. ''See, we do have something to offer,'' he proudly assured.

Kelly liked the island and realized just how glad she was that they hadn't found a hotel in Nassau. There, she would've spent her days lolling around the pool or beach, her nights in discos or nightclubs, for lack of anything else to do. Now, without a doubt, she knew she was in for exciting days with Mike, and with a warm tremor she felt the nights might turn out to be even more interesting.

They reached the hotel, and Kelly saw Edie's book laying by the rocking chair but she was nowhere around. ''I'll go see if she's taking a nap.''

Kelly found the note on the dresser. ''Gone exploring. See you at dinner. Have a wonderful day.''

When she told Mike they'd have to postpone introductions, he said, ''Well, it's a small island. We might run into her when we're doing some exploring of our own.''

They went to his dive shop, where he gave her a brief rundown of what kind of equipment she'd be using when they got started on her lessons the next morning.

"I always start beginners off in the cove," he explained. "I know every inch of that place, and there are some deep drop-offs where you can get a taste of scuba diving while still feeling like you're just in a big swimming pool."

"And when do I graduate to the ocean and that underwater cave you're talking about?"

"When you've had a few dives. I usually don't take anybody down unless they're well on their way to being certified."

Kelly was impressed and excited. "So tell me what I've got to do to get myself certified."

First of all, he said she'd have to fill out the standard diver enrollment and medical history form, then read, understand, and sign an insurance disclaimer. "I'll have to make sure you can swim two hundred yards or more and do a few other water skills test. There'll be some sessions on equipment, theory, physics, physiology, and practice of diving. Then we'll have our training and practice sessions in the cove. Then you'll have to have five or more practice dives in open water. Finally, you'll have to pass a practical and written examination, and then you'll get your certificate."

Kelly frowned. It was starting to sound complicated with lots of time involved and she said so.

"Ah, but remember . . ." he flashed a warm, flirting smile, "you'll be my star pupil. *Teacher's pet!* You'll get my undivided attention."

"Yeah, but we haven't discussed your pay," she stepped away from him, pretending to be indignant. "How do I know you won't expect a little *payola* for all that special treatment?"

It started out as a game, as he gave a mock leer and reached out to fiercely pull her against him and whisper, "Why, my dear, I thought you knew! That's part of the deal!" But as he held her close against him, the frolic ended as intense awareness took over. Eyes searching hers, he was suddenly compelled to ask, "Tell me, is there anybody special back home?"

She tensed. "Why do you ask?"

"I'd just like to know if I'm trespassing on somebody else's property."

"Nobody owns me," she crisply informed. And it was true. She'd made no promises to Neil. Any commitment *he* felt was of his own design and making. Not hers. And as for Neil being someone special, well, for the time being, he wasn't anything, because she was still angry with him. Besides, in her way of thinking, there was really nothing to tell. "I'm a free agent . . . a free spirit!"

"I knew you had lots of spirit from the start," he said, amused. "And feisty, too! I've been called lots of things by lots of women, but nobody ever accused me of being a *pervert!*"

"Sorry about that," she said lightly, somewhat disconcerted by his closeness, the look in his eyes, and the fact that his arms were still around her. Deciding to do a bit of probing herself, she asked, "And how about you? I'll bet you've got lots of beach bunnies trailing around after you."

"Afraid not," he murmured, thinking how beautiful she was, how much he wanted to kiss her. "Who wants to get tied up with a beach bum?"

"I don't consider you a beach bum . . ." She could feel the warmth of his breath on her face, and if he didn't soon let her go, she was going to melt then and there in his arms. Never could she remember a man affecting her so intently with just an embrace.

He continued to hold her, to devour her with his eyes as he spoke in a half-whisper, "Some people see me like that, I'm afraid, because I live in a little shack on an island and just take one day at a time. Some people consider that irresponsible.'' He wasn't yet ready to confide to her that the dive shop was just one of a string he owned in the Bahamas. He'd found the image of being somewhat bohemian was an aura people expected in his line of work. And besides, he wanted whatever she felt for him to be based entirely on him as an individual, not achievements in his business ventures.

Kelly murmured in all honesty, ''It sounds wonderful to me. Frankly, I envy you.''

They fell silent. It was as though an invisible curtain had fallen to wrap them in a world of their own as they silently accepted each other as kindred souls in a search for peace and tranquility from a world of conformity and judgment.

When, at last, he could resist no longer and lowered his mouth to hers, she yielded to the wildly pulsating emotions within. Dizzily, as she clung to him, Kelly knew that something strange and wonderful was happening, knew that she had to ride out the wave to discover where it crested.

Mike was on fire. He didn't want to move too fast, frighten her away by making her think passion was the root of his interest in her. *Yes, hell,* he wanted her, ached to have her, but it was much more than that. In such a short time, he found her more enjoyable, more fun to be with, than any girl he'd ever known before. And this time, he wasn't going to make any mistakes. His world was different from what she was used to, and if she learned to care for him, it had to be because she accepted that world. He would paint no rosy picture, make no golden promises.

Her lips parted for his hungry, probing tongue. She clung to him, pressed her body against his. Finally, both of them breathless and shaken, he released her to stand back and gaze down at her in reverent wonder.

At last, he placed an arm about her shoulders, began to steer her towards the door. "I think," he said raggedly, hoarsely, "we'd better head for the cove and a swim to cool off."

Kelly knew it would take more than a swim to cool off the passion that had ignited between them so quickly. Yet, she was strangely not apprehensive, for it all seemed so natural, and normal . . . and *wonderful*.

FIVE

Mike had a Moped of his own, and they rode side by side to the cove. Kelly was touched by the way he struggled to hold Biscuit in his arms so the dog wouldn't have to use his injured paw. He obviously loved the dog very much.

She couldn't help but bitterly recall how she'd never been allowed as a child to have a pet of her own. Her mother had argued she wasn't responsible enough to take care of an animal. So Kelly had joined the 4-H club and gone on field trips to farms and delighted in being around all kinds of animals. Verna had a fit over that. *"Farm clubs,"* she criticized, were beneath their social position in life. Kelly should, she dictated, devote her time to service groups, like the Candy Stripers, who wore cute pink and white uniforms and volunteered to work a few hours every week at the hospital, passing out mail to patients, pushing the carts that sold candy and magazines and toiletries. Kelly balked. She had nothing against volunteer work. It was certainly worthy, but not for Verna's reasons—which were to *see* and *be seen* socially.

Kelly had loved her 4-H work, but even when she began to win all kinds of awards, her mother still refused to allow her a dog or a cat. By then, she'd started having her asthma attacks and said animal hair would only bring them on. Kelly didn't believe that, not when the only time she seemed to have them was when she didn't get her way about something.

As they breezed along, the cool air in her face, her ash blonde hair blowing in the wind, Kelly looked from the sapphire sky to the azure ocean with the beautiful pink sand between and thought how she'd never known such peace in her entire life. Beside her, Mike turned his head to flash an infectious grin, communicating his own satisfaction with the world around him. He was, she mused, the most spirited man she'd ever met. In just the little while they'd known each other, she could tell he was every bit as fun-loving and adventuresome as she was. There was probably nothing he would not be willing to try in order to sample everything this wonderful world had to offer, and that certainly matched her own philosophy.

They reached the cove, beautifully mysterious in its quiet isolation. As they got off the Mopeds, watching as Biscuit quickly limped to the shade of a palm and laid down, Kelly wanted to know, "Just how did you come to find this place? What drove you to the life of a hermit?"

He'd been asked that question so many times by so many women; most of the time he gave a vague answer. With Kelly, though, he felt the need to share some of his past. "I guess you might say for awhile, I was a drop-out when it came to life in general. My father is a lawyer with a good practice in Boston. My mother can prove her ancestors came over on the Mayflower. You know the type. Blue bloods and proud of it." He gave a shrug to demonstrate he wasn't impressed.

"Country Clubs. Dinner parties. Always concerned about what other people think. Out-do the neighbors. That's their lifestyle. Not mine."

They went to sit down beside Biscuit, and Kelly rubbed his head affectionately as Mike talked on. "So I was a big disappointment to them, I'm afraid. Dad wanted me to go to law school, but I opted for a degree in Physical Education because I like sports. I did, however, make them happy by marrying a very proper Radcliffe graduate they whole-heartedly endorsed. They even gave us the down payment on a big house for a wedding present. Then, when all the excitement of the wedding was over, the trouble started. Teachers don't make big salaries, not enough to keep up with the Joneses, anyway. I couldn't afford the country club set. Adrian wasn't about to work to help out, and when I found out she was taking money from her folks, I blew my gourd. Things got worse then."

He fell silent, overcome with the bitterness he'd tried to escape. Kelly touched his hand in a gesture meant to convey that if he didn't want to continue, she'd understand. He was suddenly struck by the realization of how easy it was to talk to her, to confide things he usually kept locked tightly inside. He went on to admit how he'd almost become involved with one of the unmarried teachers at the school where he was working. "That's when I knew something had to give. I didn't want an affair," he said adamantly. "I didn't want to be like other guys I knew who stayed in a miserable marriage, pretending everything was great, while they fooled around on the side. Not me. I hate that kind of hypocrisy."

When he again fell silent, as though locked in his painful lament, Kelly was moved to say, "You don't have to tell me all this. It's really none of my business."

He gave a bitter laugh and continued, "Oh, it doesn't bother me to talk about it now, but I sure felt like the world's biggest fool back then. When I asked her to go with me to a counselor to see if we could work things out, she confessed she'd been having an affair with her dentist."

"Oh, no!" Kelly gasped in pity.

"Oh, *yes!* She said she just couldn't carry the guilt any longer. She'd been trying to get up the nerve to tell me she was in love, and how he'd already split with his wife so they could get married."

"So you gave her the divorce."

"Gladly. And I didn't pay her dental bill, either," he testily added.

"It must've been a rough time."

"No," he said simply, shaking his head. "Like I said, I felt like a fool for awhile, but then it dawned on me how I never really loved her, anyway. She'd been hand-picked for me by my parents. The way we were living wasn't even the kind of lifestyle I wanted, but it took me awhile to realize that because it was the way I'd been brought up, you see—that it was the proper way to live. Can you understand that?"

She nodded mutely, bitterly thinking how well she did understand!

"So that's when I decided I wanted to take a vacation to just get away and do some serious thinking about my life. I booked a cruise for a month. The last port was in the Grand Caymans, and I got off the ship there and just bummed around awhile. Didn't want to go home. Couldn't figure out at that point just *where* home was. To pass the time, I took a diving course and got the fever. I wound up going back to Boston long enough to sell the house and furniture and pack up and get the hell out of there."

"And how did you come to settle here? On Harbour Island?"

"It needed a dive shop," he said with a careless shrug.

Kelly thought it fascinating, envied his zest and enthusiasm. "Any regrets?" she wanted to know.

"Not a one. I'm happier than I've ever been in my whole life. I've made a lot of friends in the islands, and I don't have to be alone unless I want to be."

"Hey, man, I can dig that!" she cracked in her best hippie dialect, then sobered to ask, "But what about your parents? If they're like mine, they'll never give up trying to run your life."

"They don't have any choice, really. Oh, they come down maybe once a year, and my mother shakes her head and reminds me how unhappy I've made them, but I have to say we probably get along better now than we ever have. They've finally had to realize it's *my* life, and that I succeeded in cutting the umbilical cord."

Kelly didn't say so, but she felt *her* umbilical cord was wrapped around her neck, choking, and probably always would be!

He stood, reached to pull her up beside him. "Enough gloom and doom about the past. How about that swim?"

"You're on!" she cried, quickly stripping off her shirt and shorts to the bikini she'd worn beneath. Without waiting for him, she ran across the pink sand and on into the crystal blue water, plunging forward in a racing dive as soon as it reached her knees.

Behind her, he was yelling, "Hey, wait for me!" Jerking off his T-shirt, he followed in cut-off jeans.

It became a race as Kelly showed off her prowess in the water, but Mike was easily able to keep up with strong, powerful strokes. At last, he reached out to grab her and pull her beneath the surface, liking the feel of his hands running along her body, her tiny waist, and smooth, curvaceous hips. They lunged upwards, arms about each other, kissing only briefly before gulping in cool, sweet air. Kelly delighted in the taste of his salty lips, continued to press herself against him, arms entwined about his neck.

"I'm going to like being teacher's pet," she flirted.

"That makes two of us," he kissed her again until they were breathless, then reluctantly pulled away. The feel of her practically naked against him was maddening. Leery of moving too fast, too soon, he sought to get his mind on something else. "Show me some basic strokes. You know—breast, side, back. Then do a surface dive, and I'll go under with you to see how you do below."

She obliged, easily, and when they surfaced once more, he decreed she'd passed her first test—demonstrating her confidence in the water. "Tomorrow, we'll bring some equipment out here and give you your first lesson."

She wanted to know if everyone who requested an excursion was skilled. He shook his head. "No, and I have to try to weed out those who aren't so I'll know where to take them. I've got a standard dive off my boat that gets them down to a nice coral reef. There's no real danger, and they go home satisfied."

"What are the dangers?" she pressed as they treaded water to keep afloat.

He didn't quite know where to begin and said so, explaining, "Lots of things can happen, Kelly. Air embolism is considered the worst, I guess. It's caused by coming up too fast and over expanding the lungs by excessive air pressure. You never want to surface faster than your bubbles.

"Of course, drowning is also a danger," he continued. "Over eighty-five percent of all diving deaths are caused by drowning, but it's usually the direct result of something else going wrong—failure of the breathing regulator or air supply, loss or flooding of the mask, or mouthpiece. Surface exposure to rough water. Over-exertion. Exhaustion. Heart failure. Anything can happen—and does. That's why it's important to know what you're doing and keep your head. And most of all, don't goof around or take chances. My cardinal rule is never to take a group of divers down that are clowning around. It's dangerous down there. No place to get crazy."

"And sharks?" she wanted to know. "Since *Jaws*, everybody thinks about sharks!"

He couldn't help a chuckle, even though the subject was quite serious. "Sooner or later, most salt-water divers will encounter a shark, and that's a milestone in their diving career, believe me. It's a good test of enthusiasm because if a diver goes back down again after he sees one the first time, then it's in his blood. He's a born diver.

"But," he was quick to point out, "sharks aren't the only thing to watch out for. There are plenty of creatures below who don't take kindly to intruders—barracuda, eels, sting rays, jellyfish. The list goes on and on." He cocked his head to one side, appraising her reaction. "Still want to try?"

"Of course." She gave her long hair a toss, then pushed it back from her face. Not only did she suddenly want to experience what it was like to scuba dive, she knew she also wanted to take instructions from this handsome guy who so easily set her pulses to racing.

"Come on. Race you to shore." He struck out, taking long, forceful strokes.

Accepting the challenge, Kelly dove down to skim along the bottom, making better speed. When she passed him, only because he let her, they were in waist deep water, and he easily reached down to grab her and pull her up and into his arms.

"Little sea nymph," he whispered huskily, before claiming her mouth in yet another salty kiss that left both of them gasping and shaken.

At last, they reached the beach. She saw he was aroused, diverted her eyes and felt a touch of embarrassment as well as a thrilling rush.

"It's late," he said, wanting to think of anything except how much he wanted her. "How about a beer or glass of wine? I've got both at my place. Then I'll ride with you back to the hotel, and I can meet your grandmother."

"Fine, but don't *dare* refer to Edie as my *grandmother*. We adore each other, but she can't stand being thought of as anyone's granny!"

"Deal!"

He led her up the path to what he called his "hut." As they climbed, lush vegetation pressed in from both sides. Waxy dark green leaves of breadfruit alternated with the delicate tracery of coconut-palm fronds and banana leaves.

Kelly liked the little house at first sight. It had a pink-tiled roof, with white stucco walls, wood-shuttered windows that were now open for the cooling ocean breeze. There was a small garden, and she delighted in the natural stone pond. Tropical fish in a myriad of colors were easily visible in the clear depths. A waterfall trickled over rocks at one end. There were bright red hibiscus and wild orchids in lavender, pink, and white, as well as waxy anthuriums, and trailing yellow and red roses everywhere. Hand-carved wood benches afforded pleasing views of everything. Three macaws and a parrot, obviously all tame, stared down curiously at the stranger in their midst.

"It's gorgeous!" she gasped. "And you did this all yourself?"

Proudly, he admitted, "Everything. I let my imagination run wild when I started building this place. Come on inside." He opened the door, stood back for her to enter.

There was one large room, furnished in rattan furniture—a sofa, lounge chair, a table made from a cypress knee and topped with glass. A grass mat covered the floor. Nets and glass balls hung for decor, as well as several seascapes. A small kitchen was in one corner, separated by a serving bar with stools. On one side, a curtain gave privacy to sleeping quarters and a bathroom. French doors opened out to a stone terrace and yet more gardens that gave a breathtaking view of the ocean on the other side.

Mike had gone to the refrigerator, poured them both a glass of white wine. "Well, how do you like my little shack?"

"Hardly a shack, Mike, by anybody's definition. It's beautiful." She sipped the wine. It was good. He had great taste in many things, she found.

Casually and naturally, he slipped his arm about her waist as they stood on the terrace gazing into forever. "There's a full moon tonight. I've got steaks in the fridge and a grill stashed down on the beach. How about having a cook-out down there? We can even go for a moonlight swim."

He nuzzled her neck with his lips, and she felt the familiar thrilling rush once more. It sounded wonderful, and she knew she'd like nothing better—but was also aware she couldn't abandon Edie for the entire evening. She explained that, reminding, "I've left her by herself all day. And I think it'd be kind of rude."

Though he'd have preferred they be alone, he politely

suggested, "Well, how about if we ride back into town and ask her to join us? I'll scare up an extra steak."

Kelly was impressed with his generosity. "That's very nice of you, Mike."

He took the glass from her hand, set it down, along with his, then drew her into his arms. "In case you haven't noticed by now, young lady, I happen to like you. A lot. And I plan to monopolize every second of your time while you're on this island. And if it means bringing *Grandma* along once in awhile, I can handle that."

She giggled at his saying "Grandma," knew he was teasing her. "You're going to be really surprised when you meet Edie, Mike. She's not the grandmother type, and—"

He silenced her with a kiss that tasted of warm sweet wine, never wanting to let her go. She clung to him, wanting more of his tongue probing her own, delighting in the feel of the way their bodies curved together. She could feel the swell of his desire against her as invisible fingers danced in that most private place, making her tremble with want.

The gentle roar of the breakers against the rocks below pounded in unison with the wild beating of their hearts. Kelly could not remember ever wanting a man more but not just any man—*this* man, with his laughing eyes and scintillating wit, and the way he made her feel so precious and cherished with just a glance or a touch. She wanted him inside her, to possess her and take her to that special place where the tide of passion would surge and drown and deliver them both to a mystic utopia of ecstasy and fulfillment.

He moaned, deep in his throat, withdrew his mouth to cover her face with tiny kisses at the same time his hands seemed everywhere at once. He clutched at her breasts, touching the cherry pit hardness of her nipples.

He moved downwards, to slip probing fingers inside her bikini to entwine her pubic hair, to slide on further to feel her moisture, knew then she wanted him every bit as much as he wanted her. But he didn't want it like this. Not in a frenzy. He was aching in his gut and burning in his loins, but he wanted time to savor the experience, to make sure her pleasure equalled his own. He wasn't about to rush through it all in heated passion. Mustering every ounce of self-control he possessed, he released her. "I think we'd better finish our wine and ride back to town, before we get side-tracked."

With her hand shaking, Kelly reached for her glass, quickly tossed down the rest of the wine. He turned away, but she was all too aware of his erection. And, despite her own arousal that left her limp and agitated, she appreciated his understanding that she needed to get back.

They didn't talk on the ride back to the hotel, each dealing with their emotions in their own special way. Now and then, however, they would exchange a look, a smile, that plainly transmitted their growing affection for each other—as well as the ever-smoldering desire.

Edie was sitting on the porch with her book, and at once looked up with interest to see her granddaughter arriving on a Moped. She was not in the least surprised to see there was a young man beside her, and a very handsome young man, too, she decided quickly enough.

Brightly, Kelly made the introductions. "Mike, this is Edie. Edie, Mike. He's a dive instructor. Has his own shop. He's going to give me snorkeling and scuba lessons, beginning tomorrow."

Edie held out her hand to him, did a quick appraisal and decided he really was a hunk. "That sounds like something Kelly would do," she affably told him. "But I warn you. Kelly is a thrill-seeker. Always has been. You make sure she behaves herself. She's not the world's most obedient when it comes to following orders, anyway."

"Edie!" Kelly gave her a mock frown. "You know who you're starting to sound like, don't you?"

Edie's eyebrows shot up, and she waved her book at her menacingly, though there was the play of a smile on her lips. "Don't you dare say it!"

Kelly held up her hands in surrender. "Okay, okay. By the way, I didn't mean to desert you today. We came by earlier, but you were gone."

Mike chimed in to explain, "She took care of my dog this morning, when he got some glass in his paw. I took her to lunch to say thanks, and then we went for a swim at my place."

Edie nodded. "That's Kelly. She's always helping animals that need it. She even carries a bag of dog food in the back of her Bronco, so if she sees a stray that looks like he's starving, she can stop and give him something to eat."

Kelly was embarrassed. "You make me sound like the Mother Theresa of the animal kingdom."

"Is that so terrible?" Mike gave her an admiring glance, then noted, "You drive a Bronco! That's unusual for a girl."

"You'll find that Kelly *is* unusual!" Edie couldn't resist quipping.

Kelly decided it was time to get the subject off of her and bluntly asked, "So where did you disappear to all afternoon? I found your note."

Airily, Edie replied, "Oh, I had a nice time. Took a walk. Looked around."

Kelly thought she seemed a bit defensive, told herself she was imagining things, and rushed to inform Edie of Mike's invitation for the evening. "Doesn't that sound like fun?"

"And you don't even have to ride a Moped," Mike

cut in, "I've got a Jeep parked down at the shop. It's not much, and you might have a rough ride, but we'll put you up front, so it won't be so bad."

"Very nice of you, Mike," Edie acknowledged, then surprised them both by declining, going on to explain with a vague smile of regret, "I'm afraid I outdid myself today, and I'm tired. I was already feeling guilty about wanting to go to bed early with my book. You two just go ahead and have a good time."

"Are you sure?" Kelly asked suspiciously, wanting to be sure she wasn't just being polite, afraid of being a fifth wheel.

Edie gave a firm nod. "Don't worry about me. I'm going to have a wonderful evening."

Kelly looked at Mike, saw the way he was caressing her with his eyes, and knew he was secretly relieved their invitation hadn't been accepted, just as she knew *their* evening was also going to be wonderful.

Edie watched them go back to their Mopeds, smiling to herself. She wasn't about to share *her* special secret! She was just relieved it had been so easy to get rid of Kelly for the night. She had planned to plead a headache after supper, then slip out by the back stairs, cut through the alley, and then go down to the waterfront. Now, however, she reflected with a pleased smile, she had time for a leisurely bath, a nice Yellowbird in the bar . . . before meeting Captain Grady at his boat for a moonlight ride!

SIX

Mike gathered ingredients for a tropical salad from the refrigerator: mangoes, breadfruit, guavas, papayas, and bananas. Kelly got busy slicing everything into a huge bowl.

He made them a drink in his blender, and after only one sip Kelly exclaimed, "Delicious! What's in it? I can taste the rum, and the coconut, but there's something else. I want your recipe."

"No can do!" he said firmly but pleasantly. "It's my own special island drink, and the secret stays *on* the island."

"Okay," she pretended to pout, "but I was going to open up a bar back home and give you a percentage of the profits on your drink."

"Don't need the money bad enough to sell it." He looked at her thoughtfully as she stood at the sink, her back to him, finally couldn't resist asking, "Have you ever thought of just getting away from all the hassle with your folks, starting a new life like I did?"

"Sure I have, lots of times," she admitted, then, not wanting to be gloomy, merrily added, "but I was always afraid if I got too far from civilization, I'd have junk food withdrawal pains, *despite* all the great food you've got around here.''

''They've got all that in Nassau. No problem. You can be assured of your daily fix of cholesterol and fat.''

''Movies?'' she challenged. ''I'm a junkie there, too. And don't try to tell me about dozens of video stores. There's nothing like seeing a film on a wide screen, and I've yet to have popcorn at home as good as you get at the cinemas.''

''No problem. Nassau gets first-run at several theaters.''

''Cable?'' She glanced at him with playful eyes.

He threw up his hands. ''Okay. You got me there. But so what? Who wants to be a couch potato, anyway? I get the latest news from the station in Nassau with the antenna I've got on my roof, so I'm able to keep up with what a rat race the world's become. Crime on the uprise. Drugs. Inflation. I get it all, and it reinforces my satisfaction with life here.''

''Property taxes?''

''There's not any on income or inheritance. There's a little on improved property, but none at all on unimproved. The Bahamas are fortunate government costs are mostly paid for by customs revenue.

''We've got everything anybody could need, Kelly,'' he went on to assure, ''and frankly, I don't miss a thing from back home. I doubt you would, either. You don't strike me as the sort who has to be constantly entertained.''

She assured him she wasn't. ''And I have to admit your way of life *is* appealing, and it's only my second day here, and I can't help wondering if a city gal like me could ever adjust.''

''What about your family? If you're close-knit, you'd probably get real homesick.''

"That's a laugh. I can't remember a time in my life when there wasn't an argument going on about something I was doing they didn't like. For instance, they had their hearts set on my becoming a doctor, and when I switched to vet school, you'd have thought I'd been convicted of a felony."

"They accepted it eventually, didn't they?"

She mused on that, then shrugged. "I don't think *accept* is quite the right way to put it. *Tolerate* is more like it."

"Well, if you're happy where you are, that's all that counts," he said matter-of-factly. "Bloom where you're planted, as they say. Me, I found it all here, and here is where I'm going to stay." *Even if I have to go it alone,* he silently avowed, the thought making him a little blue.

He took a bag of charcoal from the cabinet under the sink, then said he was going down to the beach to start the grill. "I've got a big basket we can pack everything else in and take it down when it's time to put on the steaks."

"Plates? Knives? Forks?"

"Already packed in another basket, along with a cloth and wine glasses. I'm an old hand at this," he added with a wink as he headed out the door. "I promise to deliver a first-class gourmet picnic on the beach in the moonlight. It don't get no better than that, sweetheart!' " Another wink and he was gone.

Kelly walked to the door to watch him as he headed down the path. Why did she suddenly feel a spark of jealousy to know moonlight picnics seemed to be a regular event around here? She was foolish to think a handsome guy like Mike Kramer didn't have lots of women chasing after him. Besides, it was none of her business, especially when there was someone waiting back home for her with an engagement ring.

She sighed outloud at *that* thought—what to do about Neil. The situation was even more complicated now. How could she be in love with him when she was turning to butter every time a man she'd just met looked at her?

Mike returned to finish gathering everything else, suggesting they go on down to the beach. "I want you to see the sunset. It's going to be spectacular tonight because there isn't a cloud in the sky, and the sun is going to look like it's bleeding right into the water."

She carried the basket with salad and wine, followed after him with Biscuit on her heels. As soon as they reached the beach, she checked his paw to insure there was no swelling or sign of infection. "I think you're going to be good as new, boy," she finally decreed, giving him a pat on the head.

"You've got a way with animals," Mike remarked as he spread a blanket for them on the sand. "I can tell. I'll bet you're a real good vet."

Humbly, she responded, "I try to be. I have to admit, though, that I like to work with large animals. Horses. Cows."

"There's a combined poultry and dairy farm on the island of Eleuthera, which isn't far from here, that's one of the largest in the world. We can take a ride over there in my boat one day, if you'd like, and you can look around. Who knows? They might want to give you a job."

Kelly lay down on the blanket, and when he joined her, she teased, "Do you get a commission from the government if you convince someone to move to the Bahamas?"

"Do you think I'm trying to persuade you to move down here?"

"You're sure trying to sell me on the islands," she cheerily accused.

He made his eyes round with surprise. "Oh, is it that obvious? I thought I was being subtle about it."

"About as subtle as the way you kissed me this afternoon."

"You mean . . ." he swiftly moved to place a hand on each side of her and leaned down, ". . . like this?"

His mouth claimed hers, and she twined her arms about his neck to pull him yet closer. For long, tender moments, he kissed her, as they both reveled in the instant flames of desire that so easily ignited. Slowly, he maneuvered to one side, to render her body vulnerable to his caressing hands. With one deft movement, he'd unfastened the top of her bikini and cast it away, then he lowered his lips to devour each nipple in turn.

Kelly moaned, deep in her throat, clinging to him, arching her back to move yet closer as he continued to suck hungrily, greedily. She could feel his rock-hard organ throbbing against her belly, and she moved a hand downwards to dance curious fingers along the swollen shaft in a rhythm of splendor and awe.

He lifted his mouth to trail hot kisses along her neck as he gasped, "Kelly, I want you, honey. Here. Now . . ."

She was wearing her bikini, and in answer to his need and yielding to her own reached to untie the strings in a gesture of consent. At once, he was out of his own bathing suit, and though she was ready, eager, he wanted to postpone the inevitable joy a little longer. Moving his fingers downwards, he found that swollen nuclei which he sought, began to massage in a slow, circular movement that made her gasp and cry outloud in a plea for release.

"Not yet, not yet," he hoarsely whispered as he nibbled hungrily at her ear lobe. "I want it to be slow and easy. I want it to be so good for you, Kelly."

He brought her almost to climax, as he experienced

his own agony from wanting her so fiercely. At last, she could stand no more, dizzily realizing that never had she been so aroused, so hungry and eager for release. Boldly, she reached down to guide him between her legs and inside her. "Now!" she commanded. "I've got to have you now—"

He entered with one mighty thrust, raising up on his hands, arms stiff, as he gazed down into her enraptured face. Her nails raked the bronzed flesh of his muscular back as ecstasy became too great to bear. Again and again, he entered her, their hips rocking to and fro in frantic eagerness. She felt the explosion coming, from deep within, and she raised her legs to wrap around his back and render him yet deeper inside her.

He could not hold back his own climax, and they crested together in an explosion that sent them soaring all the way to the sunset melting into the water, then rocked them gently back to the warm and tranquil beach.

Mike looked at her in wonder, her face bathed in the fading glow of sunset. "I didn't know it could be like this."

And never, Kelly realized with a start, had she ever felt so shaken by lovemaking. Every nerve in her body was raw with keen awareness of this man who had given her pleasure like no other. Even then, she knew the ashes were still aflame, would ignite again with easy provocation. But though she wanted him, knew he would also be quickly moved for more of the same glory, she wanted, *needed*, time for retrospection. What was it about him that set her blood, her heart, on fire?

He was still on top of her, and, placing the palms of her hands against his broad shoulders, managed to speak above the roaring within. "I think we need to take a swim to cool off."

"That sounds like a winner," he agreed, awestruck

with the strange whirling of emotions. He'd had plenty of women but never one that affected him like this. He had promised himself to keep a tight rein on his heart and not get his hopes up that a meaningful, lasting relationship could come out of a summer romance. Yet his resolves were melting like the sun into the sea.

They raced to the water, plunging in and reveling in the coolness. They dove down, delighting in the wonder of the light playing among the crystal depths, then found their way into each other's arms to surface in yet another soul-shattering kiss.

When, at last, he could force himself to let her go, he knew he had to do something to lighten the tension that was grabbing like kelp and seaweed in a shallow dive. "Hey, are you sure you don't want to move down here? I'll let you live with me and be my housekeeper *and* my mistress. Biscuit needs a vet around, too. What do you say?"

She reached to put her hand on top of his head and push him under the water. When he bobbed up again, he coughed and gasped, pretending to be choked, and she feigned indignity and cried, "You're nothing but a male chauvinist! How come I have to be your mistress? How about me putting you on salary like a gigolo, pay you for your services—"

"Shut up and come here!" he growled, placing a firm hand on the back of her neck and jerking her against him for yet another sizzling kiss. They sank beneath the surface once more, the water was not very deep there, and their toes touched bottom almost at once, sending them bouncing back up into the mystically peachy light that was all that remained of the never-to-be-forgotten day.

Their eyes met and held in a gaze of wonder and adoration that made Kelly tremble in its intensity. Too much, too fast? She was not sure where the feelings were going to take her, knew only that she desperately had to take the ride.

"You . . . you promised me a steak," she said finally, forcing a laugh. "And here you are, trying to seduce me in the water."

"Who's seducing who? Come on. I'll put you to work."

They swam ashore, and they sipped cool wine while he expertly grilled the steaks. The moon slowly rose in the tranquil sky to cast silver glimmers upon the water, making ripples like thousands of tiny diamonds dancing among the gentle waves.

They enjoyed the magic around them as they slowly nibbled at the steaks neither really wanted. Then they lay side by side on the blanket, still naked, staring up into the dazzling cloak of night, alive with a thousand stars twinkling down. They held hands, each reveling in the wonder that transpired, knowing they would again make love, and that it would, once more, leave them wonderfully shaken. Yet they postponed that wonderful moment, instead wanting to share their hearts and minds and very souls to make the encounter yet a deeper blending and melding of spirits, more than just bonding of flesh.

"If I had a son," Mike began slowly, drawing upon his own private musings, "and he came to me and said, 'Dad, what should I do with my life? What should I *be* in this life?' I'd say to him, 'Son, go out and find something you enjoy doing. Don't worry about how much money you'll make doing it. Because if you enjoy your work, you'll be good at it, and when you're good at something, you're bound to make money at it.' "

Kelly could not resist a derisive snicker. "Not one time in my whole life did my parents ever come close to saying anything like that to me. They dictated what they wanted for me, especially my mother. My father just went along with anything she wanted because that's the way he is.''

"And your grandmother?"

Kelly smiled in the lustrous darkness. "We're a lot alike. Both rebels in our own way, I guess. But Edie stands up to things. I guess I'm a coward. I run.''

He rolled on his side, saw in the moonlight the sadness mirrored on her lovely face. Trailing a fingertip lovingly down her cheek, he gently advised, "You can't run from life, Kelly. You've got to face up to it head-on. It's like picking roses. Go at it slowly, cautiously, and you get pricked by a thorn. Reach in and grasp, and you're less likely to get hurt.''

Bemused, she asked, "But wasn't that what you were doing when you moved here? Running from your life back there, in that other world?"

"No, not at all," he chuckled, amused by her rationale. "Leaving all that behind was my way of facing it head-on. I came right out and admitted that wasn't the life for me. I didn't run. I *walked*. And I've never regretted one single step of the way.''

"It worked for you. It wouldn't work for everyone."

"Everyone has their own demons to deal with. They have to do it in their own way. I just happen to feel it's best to face a situation, deal with it, then put it behind you and get on with your life.''

She nodded, more to herself than in assent to his statement. Kelly knew he made sense, just as she knew she had to find some answers to her own predicament and situation in life. But he was nuzzling her neck with warm lips, and his fingertips were playing with her nipples, sending rivulets of desire coursing through her body. She couldn't think of problems then, or solutions, only the fact that once more the embers of desire were quickly igniting into raging flames, and she moved eagerly against him, melding her body against his.

"I want you, Kelly," he said, rolling her over on her back. "Here. Now. Always."

She tensed, but only momentarily. *Always.* That was the word that triggered the apprehension. Always meant forever, and forever meant his world, and it was much too soon to contemplate anything so serious or constricting. Pushing the concept of *always* way, way back into the farthest recesses of her mind, she instead yielded to wicked, wanton passion, with no restraints or bridle. Gently pushing him to lie on his back, she lifted herself to straddle him. "*My* turn!" she said boldly, happily, giving her long hair a toss in expression of her wild, abandoned freedom. Raising herself up on her knees, she reached between her thighs to feel his swollen member once more, impaling herself.

He clasped her waist and groaned between clenched teeth, "Good God, Kelly, you're driving me crazy!"

He began to meet her thrusts, but she was in control. It was *her* turn to deliciously tease, tantalize, and torment. Not only was she moving up and down but also undulating her hips, using muscles within she'd never known she possessed to rhythmically squeeze against him, then release.

She could see his face in the silver glow as he threw his head back against the sand, eyes half-closed in dazed ecstasy. He was gasping, and so was she, and her movements were coming faster. He cupped her breasts, squeezed, but she wanted more than that, wanted to feel his lips suckling. Leaning forward, she guided her breast into his mouth, and he began to lick and devour, thrusting his hips harder against her.

At last, she could not hold back any longer, and with a cry of joy, Kelly rode him to the crest, and then he grabbed her to roughly swing her over on her back to take himself to his own pinnacle of near anguished pleasure.

Finally, they lay silent in each other's arms, bodies slick with sweat.

Kelly had always dreamed of lovemaking that way, taking the initiative and command. Yet in the past, even with Len, she'd succumbed to being passive, always yielding to the missionary position. But here, tonight, with sex so new between the two of them, she had shocked herself by her boldness, but it had left her with a good, good feeling. She smiled, felt warm wonder flowing through her veins as he held her so very tightly, as though he never wanted to let her go.

Mike was in his own state of reverent awe. Other women had been as adventuresome, but never had he felt such abandonment. He liked Kelly's spirit. No, he realized with a start—he *loved* her spirit. She was unlike anyone else he had ever known, and it was exciting to think how much there was yet to discover about her. He also sensed that with each new awareness, the bond between them was going to grow. Resolve fused by past mistakes was fading like the moonglow behind the gathering clouds, yielding to hope and the slowly-budding dream that this just might be what destiny had in store for him. And he liked that thought, that theory. He intended to ride it out like one long wave', and when, at last, it crested, exploded upon the shore, if fate so decreed, then it would be like the tide—eternal.

The rain drops fell softly against their bare, feverish skin. Reluctantly, they drew apart. In silence, they gathered the remnants of their picnic, not really hurrying, for what difference did it make if they were soaked?

When they got back to the house, Kelly quietly said maybe she should be getting back into town. Secretly, she wanted time alone to ponder all that had happened that enchanted day and evening.

After they both showered and dressed, he rode beside

her on his Moped back to Dunmore Town, not about to let her travel alone at such a late hour, despite the fact there was practically zero crime on the island.

They kissed good-night on the steps of the hotel, and Kelly fervently told him, "Everything was wonderful tonight, Mike. I wish it didn't have to end."

"It's just beginning," he grinned, giving her one last kiss. "See you in a little while."

She watched him go, then went inside to try to sort out the turmoil within. Of one thing she was certain— she wanted to spend as much time as possible with Mike Kramer.

SEVEN

Edie was still sleeping when Kelly left the hotel before eight the next morning. She was starting to feel guilty about abandoning her and left a note under her door saying so. She promised to return for lunch and suggested they spend the afternoon together.

She rode the Moped to the cove, where Mike was waiting. At once, he grabbed her and gave her a smoldering kiss. Then, as she melted against him, he grasped her shoulders to give her a little shake as he grinned down at her. "Okay, that's it! I couldn't wait to do that, but now we've got to concentrate on other things, agreed?"

She jutted out her lower lip in a mock pout, teased, "But I thought I was teacher's pet."

"You are, believe me." He kissed the tip of her nose. "But I've also got a job to do, and that's making you a good diver so you'll feel confident down there. First things first."

He told her there were two categories of diving—snorkel and scuba. "Today, we're going to start out with snorkeling." He showed her the basic equipment. "Face mask. Your magic window to the sea. Without

93

it, the water forms around the curvature of your eyeball and creates an optical surface that distorts vision.

"The snorkel," he went on, showing her a J-shaped tube made of rubber. "One end fits in your mouth, and the other pokes up into the air allowing you to breathe air from the surface while your face is partially submerged."

He handed her then what looked like a rubber shoe with a rubber paddle attached. "These will increase your swimming efficiency as much as sixty percent, enabling you to move with the speed and agility of a fish while leaving your hands free." When he was sure she felt comfortable with the equipment, he pointed to the water and said, "Okay. Let's do it."

Walking with the fins on, she quickly discovered, was awkward. "Now I know how the Creature from the Black Lagoon felt!" she wailed, lifting her feet high off the ground to keep the blade of the fin from buckling and tripping. But when she stepped into the water, the blade did fold, and she promptly fell on her bottom with a splash.

Laughing, Mike pulled her up and explained, "You can't keep from buckling against the resistance of the water. You have to walk backwards."

Now she did feel a bit ridiculous, but there was no time to think about that because he began to instruct her on how to lower her head into the water when the water was a few inches above her waist to get used to breathing through the snorkel. He was amazed that Kelly had no difficulty at all and was quickly adapting to breathing through the tube. "Great!" he complimented. "Now let's try a surface dive."

She did a *cannonball tuck*, first hyperventilating to build up a supply of residual oxygen in her lungs, then executed a powerful backward stroke with both hands as she tucked both knees up under her chest, rolling head and shoulders forward under the water. With her hips directly over her head, she lifted her legs out so that they stuck straight up above the surface, then dove straight down.

Mike thought what great legs she had. He was also thinking what great *everything* she had, then remembered what he was supposed to be doing and promptly dove after her.

He was amazed at how quickly Kelly caught on to snorkeling. He'd planned only a short lesson for that morning, figuring most of the time would be taken up with her learning the equipment and breathing techniques. But in a short time she'd mastered it all, and he led her to snorkel among a reef just outside the cove. She was dazzled by the coral formations, marveling at him through her mask with wide, incredulous eyes.

When they surfaced, she begged for more. "It's like another world down there!" she cried exuberantly, loving the way the sun's brilliance made the gently rolling water sparkle like a million shards of glass. "I can't believe it. I've seen movies, pictures, but nothing can compare to the real thing. Why, I can see all the way to the bottom! And the colors—golds and purples and blues and greens. It's absolutely breathtaking."

"The water is pure," he explained, "because there aren't any rivers in the Bahamas to contaminate it with silt. And down below there are high plateaus that form what's called the 'Bahama Banks,' for thousands of square miles, all covered with yellow sand. The effect of the sun penetrating down to that sand, in various depths, as it reflects off the coral, creates all those different colors."

"Show me more!" she begged.

"Not without scuba gear. We'll start on that tomorrow, but right now I've got to get into town and get ready to meet a dive group booked from Nassau. Want to go with us, just to ride on my boat?"

She desperately would have liked to but explained she felt obligated to spend some time with Edie.

They swam back to shore, dried off, and after donning shorts and T-shirts rode back to the harbor on their Mopeds. This time, Biscuit trotted happily alongside. Kelly was relieved he was no longer limping.

"Dinner tonight?" Mike asked hopefully when they got to his shop.

They were outside, in the parking lot, and Kelly knew it was not the broiling sun above that made her feel so hot inside. It was his nearness, the way he made her feel as though he were touching her, caressing her, even though they stood apart. His tongue touched his dry lips, and she wanted to feel it melding against her own. He reached to brush his hair back from his eyes, and she wanted to run her fingers through the wavy thickness. He brushed sand from his shoulder, and she longed to lay her head upon it.

"Kelly?" he prodded, then laughed and waved a hand in front of her face. "Where are you?"

In your arms, she silently confided, then forced a bright smile and instead said she'd let him know later about dinner. "Edie didn't come here to sit in a rocking chair and read. I've really got to spend some time with her."

He said he'd check with her when he got back in late that afternoon, and Kelly fired up her scooter once more and headed for the Sea Gull. When she arrived, Edie wasn't on the porch, and she quickly discovered neither was she in her room or anywhere about. Reeta, the combination desk clerk and head housekeeper said she'd left early that morning and didn't say where she was going, only that she'd be back late in the day and Kelly was to have fun and not worry about her. Kelly suspected Edie had purposely disappeared, knowing she'd feel obliged to spend time with her. That was okay, if that's what she wanted, but Kelly wished she'd known sooner. Now she was stuck with nothing to do the rest of the day.

Returning to the dock, she arrived just in time to see Mike's boat, which he'd aptly christened the *Free Spirit*, chugging along towards the horizon. Even Biscuit had gone with him, so she was truly alone.

Hungry from the morning's exertion, she decided to have lunch at the Mariner. Anna heartily welcomed her, seated her at the same table she'd shared with Mike on her previous visit. It made her feel even lonelier, remembering how much they'd enjoyed themselves. Ridiculous, she chided herself. They'd had a nice afternoon, evening, and morning together, and she was acting like a lovesick schoolgirl. Still, there had been the undeniably exquisite passion, and the wonderful memories were still smoldering.

Anna persuaded her to sample the specialty of the day—green turtle pie, and Kelly was surprised to find it delicious. As she lingered over a glass of lemonade, Anna brought her check and politely asked how she liked the island. "I love it," she was quick to tell her. "Beautiful. Peaceful. A true paradise."

"And Captain Mike?" Anna prodded, a mischievous gleam in her dark eyes. "Him you like, too?"

Kelly couldn't help a fond smile as she nodded, "Yes. I like *Captain* Mike. He's teaching me to dive."

"Ah, a good teacher. He taught my little sister, Winny, just last summer, when she was only six years old. She's very good now. She and some of her friends have a diving club, and Captain Mike takes them out on excursion once a month. They love it. They love him," she added proudly.

"Six years old?" Kelly echoed. That seemed uncanny, but then these were island children, who'd grown up around the water and probably knew how to swim before they learned how to walk. "I think that's marvelous. Where is Winny? I'd like to meet her."

A shadow crossed Anna's dark face. She gave a nod towards the door leading to the kitchen. "Out there, in the storage room. Her dog, she is very sick. Dying, I think. There is nothing to be done, but she wants to stay with her."

Kelly was already on her feet and heading towards the kitchen. Anna, puzzled by her concern, but grateful, hurried after her.

A skinny little girl with beautiful brown eyes looked up as Kelly stepped into the dimly-lit room beyond the kitchen. Somehow, she sensed the pretty lady had come to offer aid. "My dog . . ." she said, tears streaming down her cheeks as she cradled a small shaggy black dog in her arms. "Can you help her, please? She is so sick."

Anna interjected, "We don't have a dog doctor on the island, and the dog . . ." she gave a helpless shrug. "She was a stray. She took up here. I have no money to spend on stray animals."

"She's not a *stray* anymore!" Winny protested fiercely and possessively. "She's my dog now!"

Kelly knelt down. The dog looked at her with dull, lacklustre eyes, gave no sign of being frightened. Gently, she ran her hands over her for any sign of injury but found nothing. Without a stethoscope, she couldn't check for heart rate but a pulse beat by fingertip appeared normal. "Has she been sick or had symptoms of an upset stomach?" she asked Winny.

Winny nodded. "Yesterday and the day before. Today, she hasn't done anything but lie there."

Kelly lightly pinched the dog's skin on her back between thumb and forefinger. She was badly dehydrated. Pulling her upper lip back from her gums, suspicion of anemia was confirmed. The gums were white, bloodless. "We need to get her to a clinic. She needs fluids." She didn't think Winny would understand if she told her about IVs. To Anna, she said, "We'll need something to wrap her in. An old towel or blanket will do. If you'll take care of that, I'll go make arrangements to get us to Nassau."

She left Winny smiling optimistically from ear to ear, but Anna was close on her heels to ask worriedly as soon as they were outside the storage room, "Do you think she can be helped? Winny loves that dog so much, and I hate to get her hopes up if there's no chance."

"I think she's got a good chance. As best I can tell without lab tests, I'd say she's just got a big case of intestinal parasites. A shot and a few pills should fix her right up."

"And how can you be sure?"

"Because I'm a veterinarian, and I've seen cases like this before. Sometimes the dog does die. But in this instance, I think we've got it in time."

Kelly was almost out the front door of the restaurant when Anna impulsively told her, "You're very nice, and I have to tell you . . ." she added with a conspiratorial wink, "I think you're the prettiest girl Mike ever brought here."

She disappeared back inside, and Kelly stared after her. *Gee, thanks,* she silently, glumly mused. That was just what she needed to hear, all right, that the Mariner was Mike's favorite place for dining with his girlfriends. No matter, she chided herself for the flash of jealousy. They had no strings on each other, and she had no reason to think what they'd shared was anything more than it was—good times, good sex. And wasn't that what she'd thought she had with Neil? The problems had begun when he took it for more than it was, and she wasn't about to make the same mistake just because she found Mike Kramer devastatingly gorgeous and the most exciting man she'd ever known.

There were several boats tied up along the main dock, and Kelly had no difficulty in hiring one to take her and Winny and the dog into Nassau. Within a half hour, they were on their way, and in another, they were entering the main channel.

Taxis were everywhere, and Kelly waved at the one closest. The driver said the nearest veterinary clinic was about a ten-minute ride. Kelly looked at the dog lying so very still in Winny's arms, hoped they were in good time. "Just hurry," she urged.

The clinic was in a building made of limestone coral rock. Mike had explained to her how the rock, taken from the ground, was soft enough to be cut with a wood saw, and once exposed to air the coral hardened with age. The roof was made of overlapping coral shingles, like so many of the other older structures in Nassau. Periodically coated with lime for cleanliness's sake, the rains that slid over the shingles could be funnelled into a reserve water tank below.

The air was sweet, as always, with the delicate scent of the flowers that seemed to be everywhere.

"Let me take her now," Kelly said, as they started up the stairs. "We don't want you to drop her."

Inside, the waiting room was filled to overflowing with people and their pets. Kelly went to the receptionist and explained she was a veterinarian herself, from the United States, and she'd brought the dog over from Harbour Island, and it was an emergency.

"I'll see what I can do," the girl got up and hurried through a door.

Kelly looked around. There wasn't a vacant seat. She motioned Winny to sit down on the floor, then handed the docile dog to her. A few seconds later, a tall, dark-skinned man in a white coat, dark trousers, breezed into the room to clasp Kelly's hand with both of his.

"I'm Dr. Brewster," he greeted enthusiastically.

"Welcome to Nassau. I'm swamped here, as you can see . . ." he made a wild gesture taking in the whole room of anxiously staring faces. "But come along. I will give you an examining room, and you can take care of the dog yourself."

He practically ran out, and Kelly was right behind him to remind she had no license to practice in Nassau. "No problem," he waved an arm in dismissal. "You just do the lab tests. I'll medicate. No problem. No problem." He shook his head firmly to punctuate.

Kelly was impressed with the modern and clean facilities, but it was obvious the clinic was vastly understaffed and overloaded with patients. Dr. Brewster gave her a quick tour, and she saw that nearly all the cages were filled with sick animals. He directed her into a small examining room, assuring she would find everything she needed if she just looked for it. Then he left her.

Winny watched with interest as Kelly got her specimen from the dog, then examined it under a microscope. She saw the parasites she was looking for. She went in search of Dr. Brewster and told him of her diagnosis. He was in the middle of taking stitches from a dog that had been spayed, absently waved her towards a supply cabinet. "Glucose. IV. You can start it. I'll be right there."

She'd just finished when he breezed in to give medication. He left her again, and there was nothing to do but sit beside the dog and wait, hoping to see some sign of improvement.

The hours passed, and when the dog lifted her head and whimpered in boredom, Kelly and Winny exchanged happy grins and hugged each other. She was going to be okay.

"Leave her here tonight if you like, and the night attendant will keep an eye on her," Dr. Brewster said when he stopped by to see how things were going. "If she's still doing okay tomorrow, take her home."

"You're very kind," Kelly gratefully told him, then assured, "I'll take care of the bill myself."

"Only for the drugs. Nothing more. You did all the work." He appraised her with admiring eyes, then dared ask, "Would you like a job here? We could sure use another doctor."

"Sorry. I'm just on vacation." She shook his hand, thanked him once more, then left with Winny in tow.

They stopped for an ice cream, then Kelly said they needed to get started back to the island. It was getting late, and Anna might be worrying.

As they walked along the cobblestone streets in the gathering dusk, headed for the main waterfront, Kelly was struck with the reality of just how *good* she felt. Seeing the scruffy little dog rally to medication was reward enough, but the happy glow in Winny's eyes added frosting to the cake. No matter she'd taken up her whole afternoon in ministering to the animal, and it was also of no consequence that she wouldn't get paid for her time and skills. The way she felt inside was payment enough, which made her think of her mother's nagging that she'd never get rich. As a *doctor*, Verna had insisted, she would make much money. To make ends meet as a *veterinarian* would mean many more long hours. Well, Kelly could argue with that point. She knew of a lot of vets who were making big bucks. It depended on the area where they practiced, the type of clients they had. Purebreds versus mutts, as it were. But financial remuneration hadn't played a part in her decision to switch careers. It was just something she wanted to do, something she knew she'd enjoy. And wasn't that what life was all about, like Mike said?

Mike.

Just thinking of him made her feel all warm inside.

What good times they had together. Laughing, loving, and just *living*. She felt so at ease with him. No pretense. No apologies for just being herself. Natural. Good. She couldn't remember being as relaxed around a man before and certainly couldn't recall having better times. Maybe it was the tropical heat, or the fantasy island atmosphere. Whatever! Kelly just knew she was having the time of her life!

Lost in her reverie, she was jolted when Winny gave her hand a tug and excitedly cried, "Look! It's Captain Mike!"

He saw them and waved, finished tying the boat to a piling, then bounded onto the pier. He looked neat, robust, in white slacks, blue pullover, dockers, and no socks. Kelly eagerly stepped into his arms for a cheerful hug. "How'd you know where we were?"

"Anna told me. She started getting worried when you all didn't come back. I called the clinic, and Dr. Brewster said you'd just left. He also said the dog is doing just fine. I decided to run over and see if I could give you a ride home."

"Very nice of you," Kelly murmured, not only grateful for his kindness but wanting very much to kiss him to demonstrate just how much.

"Later . . ." he whispered, reading her mind and squeezing her hand. "Lots of time for that later. God, I've missed you this afternoon, Kelly."

Suddenly, Winny chirped to proudly inform, "Miss Kelly, she saved my dog!"

Kelly gently corrected, "No, *I* didn't save your dog, Winny. *Medicine* did."

Winny shook her head, firmly corrected, "Not entirely so. You knew what to do. That's what counts."

"Yeah, *Miss* Kelly," Mike chimed in, giving her a playful nudge with his elbow. "That's what counts."

"And you know what I'm going to do?" Winny went

on brightly, "I'm going to name her for you. Before, I was afraid to give her a name because I didn't think they'd let me keep her, but now I know they will, and I'm going to call her *Kelly*."

"Well, Winny, I guess that's about the nicest thing anybody's ever done for me. Thank you." She exchanged an amused smile with Mike.

They got on the boat, and Mike remarked, "Maybe now you can see why we need a vet on Harbour Island. There's lots of kids there with pets, and their parents can't haul them back and forth to Nassau for check-ups and inoculations. But, sadly, there's not enough money to attract one. Maybe one day . . ." he let his voice trail, kicked the engine into gear, and they took off, slicing through the azure water.

Kelly was seated beside Winny at the rear. Her hair blew freely about her face, and she sighed deliciously. It was all so peaceful, so calm and tranquil, and she could let her mind flow and forget all the troubles and cares back home.

Mike's back was to her as he concentrated on steering the craft in the lavender shades of twilight. She saw the way his sinewy muscles rippled, the tight cords in his forearms. Powerful. Forceful. He was, she mused, quite a man, and she felt the familiar tremors of desire to recall his deliciously wonderful embrace. He turned, as though sensing her gaze, her thoughts, and he blew her a kiss, eyes holding a promise of repeated ecstasy.

Kelly closed her eyes, leaned back to revel in the kiss of the wind upon her face. She had come to this island to sort out her problems and now found herself entangled in passion, and, yes, budding romance. Where would it lead? She had no idea. She only knew that, like the waves cresting beyond the reef, she would ride with the tide to whatever destination fate had in store.

EIGHT

Edie was, for a change, waiting on the front porch. Kelly merely said she'd been to Nassau, but Mike promptly told her all about how she'd saved Winny's dog by realizing what was wrong and getting him to a clinic where IV and medication were available.

"Well, imagine that!" Edie exulted. "It just goes to show how desperately they need a vet around here."

Suspicious, Kelly asked, "And how would you know they don't have one?"

"Oh, I get around a little on my own," she airily informed, hastened to add, "I imagine it was a very rewarding experience. No doubt that child will be your friend for life."

Mike substantiated. "Absolutely. The last we saw of Winny, she was running to tell all her friends about her new pal—the super-vet! By the way . . ." he said, remembering Anna's invitation. "Winny's sister has invited all of us for dinner at the Mariner tonight as a thank you to Kelly. We'd like for you to go with us, Edie." He had sat down in the rocker beside her.

"Oh, I don't think so," Edie graciously declined.

"You two don't need a chaperone. Go on and have a good time."

At that, Kelly balked. "Wait a minute." She went to perch on the railing in front of her and sternly point out, "We haven't had any time together since breakfast the first morning we got here. I've been running off with Mike, and you've been wandering around by yourself, and that's not right. Now we want you to come with us tonight, and that's final."

Later, Kelly would recall how she'd never known Edie to display such firm resolution, almost to the point of anger. "No! I'm enjoying my book, and I don't feel like eating out. But thank you just the same."

Her tone was so sharp that even Mike glanced up at Kelly to judge her reaction, gave a shrug to indicate there was no point in arguing.

With a sigh of resignation, Kelly said she was going to get a shower, change clothes, and she'd meet him at the restaurant in an hour. "Wear something casual, like shorts or jeans," he called after her. "I thought we'd take the boat out afterwards for a ride in the moonlight."

When she came back downstairs, Edie was still sitting on the porch but not reading because her book lay closed in her lap, forgotten for the moment. Struck by her pensive, almost dreamy expression, Kelly hesitated. Finally, when she pushed the door open with a loud squeak, Edie quickly returned from wherever she'd been, to cheerily announce, "I like Mike! He's handsome and energetic and seems to have a nice personality. So how do *you* feel about him?"

She wasn't about to confide she liked him maybe too much, too soon, instead offered, "He's a great instructor. I think I'm hooked on diving."

"Then you're glad we came here," Edie probed, "instead of staying at some posh hotel in Nassau?"

"Absolutely. I'm surprised there's so much to do. Mike says he's going to take me to Eleuthera one day, to visit a huge cattle and poultry ranch they have there. He also wants to take me to St. George's Cay. It's on the northern tip of Eleuthera. There's a settlement there called the Spanish Wells, where they grow fruits and vegetables for most of the markets in Nassau, and—" She saw the way Edie was looking at her in amusement and demanded, "What's wrong?"

"Nothing's wrong. I was just thinking how I can't ever remember seeing you so happy. You're positively glowing. I can't make up my mind if it's the islands or being in love."

"Love?" Kelly echoed, stunned. "Who said anything about love? Edie, get real! I haven't known Mike but a few days, and—"

"Oh, for heaven's sake," she interrupted with an airy wave. "It doesn't matter how short a time you've known him if he makes you happy. Why don't you just let yourself go and be impulsive if you want to, and this time do so for the *right* reasons?"

"Right reasons?" Kelly was baffled. "What's your point?"

Edie spoke in a rush, as though having rehearsed exactly what she wanted to say when the opportunity came. "I'll give you the point. From the time you were born, your mother had your life all planned out for you, but as you got older, you started rebelling. The real problem came when that rebellion made you feel guilty. So, because of that guilt, you punished yourself by being almost self-destructive by doing things that were impulsive and reckless, and—"

Kelly felt the need to challenge, "Are you saying that my switching from medical school to vet school was *self-destructive?*"

"No, absolutely not. That was a wise choice. You're

a good veterinarian, and it's obvious you enjoy what you do, and I really believe it's your true calling. You probably wouldn't have made as good a doctor because your heart wasn't in it. I sensed that, but I couldn't convince your folks to seé it, too. But then you felt guilty about disappointing them and ruining *their* dream, so you punished yourself by jumping off and marrying that loser, Len. Your subconscious probably knew it would never work out.''

Kelly couldn't resist teasing, ''Have you been reading *Psychology Today* again?''

Edie wagged a finger, ''Don't be *snarty!* I'm right, and you know it, and the thing that worries me is that even though you might be starting to realize just where you made your mistakes, you're going to make another one by doing a 360-degree turnaround in every aspect of your life, and that's not wise. When it comes to affairs of the heart, sometimes a person *has* to be impulsive. Sometimes you've got to reach out and make a grab for that big, brass ring and hang on for the ride and say to hell with the consequences when the merry-go-round stops turning.''

''Whew!'' Kelly gasped. ''That was quite a roll. What's in to you lately? You've really been acting strange.''

''It's the tropics!'' Edie laughed, waving her away. ''Now be off with you. But remember what I said. Let yourself go. The clock is ticking!''

Kelly had started down the steps but hearing that turned to fearfully ask, ''When *do* we have to go back?''

Edie sobered. ''We aren't leaving till we're good and ready, but now that the subject has come up, maybe I'd better show you this.'' She took a folded yellow paper from her book that she'd been using to mark her place. ''This came from your mother this afternoon.''

"A telegram?" Kelly reached for it. "Nobody sends *telegrams* anymore, and there are phones here if she wants to call on *her nickel* to nag."

"She thinks we've left civilization entirely since we're not staying at a regular resort hotel. You know your mother. Her idea of roughing it is a *Holiday Inn.*"

Kelly laughed at that truism, but the hilarity ended as she read the terse, angry lines: *"Come home at once. Enough is enough. Neil is terribly upset, and you're breaking our hearts! How can you treat us this way when we all love you so much?"*

Shaking her head, she gave the telegram back. "This is no surprise, but what does baffle me is that she hasn't had one of her attacks and used that to try to get us back."

"Well, when you dared leave town while she was in the throes of one, I guess she's decided emotional blackmail isn't going to work anymore. If she can't victimize you with threats, or pleading Neil's case for him, she'll probably use your father next and say he's on his deathbed."

Kelly dropped to the top step to sit with head in hands, glumly staring out at what had begun as an enchanting evening but now seemed shrouded with misery. Drearily, she yielded, "Maybe we should just go on back, so I can face the music. Why postpone the misery? I'll just tell Neil the truth—that at this point in time, I just don't care enough about him to even think about marriage any time soon. Mom will rant and rave when I do, so the best thing is to quit my job, try for the one in Texas, and just get the hell away from it all for awhile, and—"

"Oh, shut up, Kelly!"

Kelly jerked around to stare at her. She had never heard her speak like that.

"You heard me," Edie snapped. "I'm sick of hearing that kind of talk. Why don't you grow up and assert yourself and stand up for yourself, instead of running away like an angry little girl?

"If Verna sends word Walter is sick," she rushed on, "I'll call his doctor directly and find out for myself if it's so. And I'll check out every trick she tries to pull. We aren't going home till we're good and ready to go, and that's the way it's going to be. Agreed?"

Kelly felt washed with relief. Edie was right. It was time she took control of her life without feeling guilty about it. "Agreed!" She leaped up to give her a grateful hug and offered, "Thanks, too, for sticking by me like you do."

"I *have* to," Edie responded with mock severity. "I feel responsible because you're just like me—a rebel! Now off with you. And hurry up and let yourself fall in love with Mike Kramer if it feels right, which will prove *me* right—*again!*"

In the restaurant, Kelly was the center of attention. It seemed Anna was related to just about everyone on the island, and they'd heard about the trip to Nassau to save Winny's dog, and they all trooped in to praise her for what she'd done. When at last the excitement dwindled, she told Mike in wonder, "For heaven's sake, I didn't do open heart surgery on the dog!"

"They're grateful for what you *did* do. After all, you are on vacation, but you took the trouble to save a little girl's pet. That's pretty neat, Kelly. I'm impressed."

Kelly couldn't help thinking how her mother would've said she was crazy, but the reality was, she *did* feel good about what she'd done, and that, she felt, was the way life was *supposed* to be!

"I like Harbour Island," she suddenly felt the urge to say. "I like the people here. I'm beginning to think I could feel at home here."

Mike reached to refill her glass with champagne,

decided it was best not to pick up on her remark. No matter that his feelings grew stronger each time they were together, any decision as to her future had to be her doing, not because he had encouraged or manipulated.

After dinner, they boarded the *Free Spirit*, standing with arms about each other as the boat moved slowly out of the harbor. The night was a curtain of black velvet above a sea flashing crystal in the moon and starlight. At last, he cut the engine but left the running lights on so they could drift along but be seen by other craft that might be in the area.

Taking her hand, he led the way below. There was a tiny galley and a double bed tucked in a corner. They sat down, and he nuzzled her neck and playfully whispered, "Want to know a secret?"

She nodded, reveling in the ardent moment.

A mischievous smile touched his lips, and his eyes were twinkling as he looked down at her and admitted, "I always carry a pair of binoculars in the Moped satchel, and I stood there that first day and watched you floating naked on the water for a long, long time before I did the gentlemanly thing and sent Biscuit out to let you know someone was around."

"Pervert!" she cried then, pretending indignity all over again. "I knew it! I'm surprised you didn't drag me out of the water and rape me right on the beach, and—"

"You mean like this?" He grabbed her and swung her down on the bed, then fell on top of her, began to yank fiercely at her clothes.

Matching his playful mood, Kelly was swept into the fantasy. She pretended to resist, rolling from side to side as he quickly unbuttoned her blouse, jerking away her bra and rendering her breasts to his assaulting lips. Almost painfully, he suckled each nipple in turn as he held her wrists pinioned above her head with one hand, his other diving downwards to yank down her shorts and bikini panties. He began to caress between her legs, to tantalize and tease her to a fevered pitch. All the while, she moaned and struggled, and he fiercely growled, "You know you want it, and I'm going to have it. You're mine, you wench, like pirate booty, and I'll have you any time I want you, and damnit, I want you now!"

He jerked off his cut-off jeans, then threw her legs up and over his back. With a mighty thrust, he was inside her, and Kelly could play the game no longer. With a shuddering cry, her nails dug into his shoulders as she locked herself against him in unison. They were as one, matching rhythmic thrusts. Kelly could not hold back her climax, which came all at once, followed by a mighty explosion as Mike's own glory erupted.

Burrowing his face in her neck, he groaned, "Dear God in heaven, it's never been like this, Kelly. What've you done to me, girl? I'm bewitched."

She clung to him, feeling enchanted, spellbound, unable and unwilling to try and put what she was experiencing into words. She could feel the thundering of his heart against her own, and in that instant wished only that time could stand still and freeze the moment forever.

At last, he rolled to one side to hold her yet tighter in his arms. "It's more than just the sex, you know," he said finally.

Kelly nodded. She sensed that in him, in herself.

"I don't know where it's going, but I intend to play it out."

Turning to face him, she trailed a fingertip down his cheek. She could see him in the pale light filtering through a porthole above the bed, and she adored the way he looked—so warm and sensuous and satisfied.

Deciding maybe it was time to be serious about a few things, she took a deep breath and dared to admit, "I'd like to play it out, too, Mike, but I think it's time I admitted it's not just a game with me where you're concerned."

He was quick to amend, "I didn't mean I was playing games, Kelly. I care about you—more than I thought I could ever care about a woman again." Maybe, the thought suddenly occurred, he'd been behaving a bit too casual with her. Propping himself on one elbow, so he could see her face in the moonlight, he revealed, "There's something you should know about me, Kelly. When I first came here, I wasn't like you see me now—settled, satisfied. I was going through a kind of culture shock, trying to get used to the changes in my life, even though I knew it was what I wanted. I hadn't made a lot of friends yet, and, frankly, I was lonesome. I guess I wore my heart on my sleeve. I met a girl on a diving expedition and let it get too serious. She conned herself, and me, into thinking she'd move down here, but when she went back to her world, that was it. A few love letters and then nothing." He gave a cynical laugh. "I'm afraid that's the way it was with a few others, too. They'd come down here on vacation and be hypnotized by the moonlight and magic, and when they went home, the romance lasted as long as their tan. So if I seem a bit flip with you, it's because I've been burned, and I'm not taking anything for granted. Can you understand that?" He searched her face for some sign that she did.

Kelly was trying to sort out her own thoughts. Finally, she was able to admit, "It's all happening fast for me, Mike. I've never felt this way about anybody before, and certainly not so soon. And it scares me."

"I'm not going to hurt you," he was quick to assure, "and you don't have to worry about me putting on pressure for you to feel something you don't. All I ask of you is honesty.''

"You've got that," she fervently told him. "And that's all I'm asking of you, too.''

He pulled her against him, and she answered his call, and they were once more caught up in a tide of passion that would only crest with the explosions of emotion that would leave them dazed with wonder. Never had Kelly wanted a man more, and never had she felt so bold and deliciously wicked and wanton.

They went up on deck to make love beneath the soft curtain of the tender night. Then Mike steered them into the cove in front of his place, where he dropped anchor so they could swim naked in the cool, star-dazzled water.

Finally, they went back onboard and realized they were both hungry. Mike showed off his skill in the tiny galley, whipping up a cheese omelet. At last, they snuggled in bed and fell asleep, waking up only when the hot, morning sun streamed through the porthole.

"Edie will think we drowned!" Kelly cried, startled. "What time is it?"

Mike glanced at his watch on the bedside table. "Nearly nine. If we'd been out in the waterway, we'd have been awakened by the sound of the fishing boats going out, but we're kind of isolated here. I can have us back in about ten minutes though.''

When Kelly was dressed, she joined him once more at the helm. They were chugging through the water at a fast pace, and the harbor of Dunmore Town loomed larger by the minute. He leaned to kiss her forehead, worriedly asked, "Will she be mad because we stayed out all night?"

She shook her head. "She's not like that. I mean, she'd never be judgmental about our sleeping together. I'm just afraid she'll be worried something might've happened. She heard you say we were taking the boat out."

He nodded, increased the speed of the engines. He didn't want Edie angry with him because he wanted only smooth sailing in his relationship with Kelly. Last night, when she'd laid sleeping in his arms, he'd stared at her lovely face in the silver moonlight and knew, without a doubt, he was falling in love. But he was also painfully aware of another given—she'd have to want to live in his world. Never could he live in hers. Not now. Not when he'd found himself and knew what he wanted in this life. All he could do now was hope and pray she was loving him, too, that she'd want to make *his* world *hers*. If not, he was in for the "Big Hurt" again—only this time, he knew it would be pain unlike anything he'd ever known before. But there was nothing he could do. Fate was at the helm of his life now.

When the boat was close enough to the pier, Kelly leaped ashore without waiting for him to tie up. She hurried the short distance to the hotel, saw the porch was empty. She went inside, looked in the dining room but didn't see Edie there, either. Rushing upstairs, she knocked on her door but got no answer.

Just then one of the maids came out of the room across the hall, and Kelly asked, "Have you seen my grandmother this morning?"

She shook her head, then flashed a tigerish grin. "You two sure make my work a lot easier."

Kelly said she didn't know what she meant.

"You didn't mess up your beds last night. I don't have hardly any cleaning to do in your rooms."

It hit her then. "You mean my grandmother's bed wasn't slept in last night?"

The maid stared at her, suddenly fearful she'd said something she shouldn't. She retreated a few steps, nervously explaining, ''I knocked on her door because she hadn't put the *Do Not Disturb* sign out. The room was empty, and the bed was still made up. I'm sorry . . .'' she continued to back on down the hall, turned, and disappeared into a linen closet.

Terror was a chilling bolt to her heart, as Kelly took off for downstairs. Something had happened to Edie! She'd probably gone for a walk last night, and, oh God! Her eyes filled with tears, and she was shaking from head to toe. She had to call the police and get out a search party, and—

She froze mid-way down the stairs.

Edie was walking into the dining room but glanced up and saw her. ''Good morning,'' she cheerily called. ''I was just out for an early morning walk and now I'm ready for breakfast. How about you?''

Kelly could only stand there, trying to figure out what the hell was going on. Had Edie, by chance, made up her own bed? Surely not. She'd figure maid service came with the room, so why bother? Yet, if she had stayed out all night, where had she been, and, more importantly, *whom* had she been *with?*

Finally, she made her way on down the steps, managed to calmly respond, ''No breakfast for me, but I could use a cup of coffee.''

''I want to hear all about the boat ride,'' Edie said breezily, as they entered the dining room.

Kelly thought how she'd like to hear about a few things, too, but now wasn't the time to ask. But, for sure, she'd keep her eyes open from now on because Edie obviously had a secret, and she intended to find out what it was!

NINE

Sun-drenched days, sweet with the perfume of the flowers and spicy with the pungent salt air, blended into magical tropical nights of stardust and splendor.

Despite all the arguments within himself, Mike knew he was falling in love. That reality, however, did not cause so much concern as did awareness this was above and beyond anything he'd ever felt for a woman before. Deep. Abiding. Yet he was tortured by screaming reminders that Kelly was of a different world—a world he had, for all intents and purposes, turned his back on for good.

When Mike had first come to the islands, he'd had less than five thousand dollars left in his bank account. There hadn't been much money, anyway, once the dust settled after the divorce. His furious parents had wanted their wedding gift of the down payment returned. He hadn't lived in the house long enough to build up an equity, so once the jumbo mortgage was paid off, along with the charge cards and other bills accumulated while trying to live the lifestyle of the rich and famous, there wasn't much left after he bolted off for his find-himself-again cruise.

His family had predicted he'd come crawling back on his knees inside of a year, which only served to make him all the more determined to prove them wrong. Sinking everything into the first dive shop he opened, which was on Harbour Island, he did so well after just the first year he was able to open two more shops during the next tourist season—one in Eleuthera and another in the Exuma Cays. Profits on those led to the birth of Neptune, Incorporated, and his territory had grown to include Andros Island, Freeport on Grand Bahama, with plans to expand into the Florida Keys before moving on further south and into the Caribbean.

So while he was well off financially, for all appearances he was no more than a beach bum. That was the image he projected, which, he privately acknowledged, was probably the *real* Mike Kramer—a man with no cares or woes, who took one day at a time and rolled with the punches and to hell with what anyone else thought. No matter that he was a member of every club in the Bahamas of merit, or that he played golf with wealthy retirees or prominent businessmen. He was happiest fishing with his native buddies from the islands, or sipping a beer or rum and Coke in the grubbiest of inlet bars. Most importantly, he felt comfortable in any social situation but didn't need status to make his way. What he did need, he was so painfully reminded as he and Kelly spent more and more time together, was to fill the empty place in his heart.

The fact that sex was the greatest with Kelly was not the dominant attraction in their relationship. That was just an added bonus because there didn't seem to be anything they didn't enjoy together. Never was there a dull moment, and the only cloud in their sky of bliss was his fear it would end. He was, however, trying to think positive, dreamed of how it might be if they did get married. They could keep the house on Harbour

Island as a retreat, but he also owned a beautiful waterfront lot in a quiet section of Nassau, where they could eventually build something larger.

Wanting Kelly exposed to all that Nassau had to offer, he set out one day for a typical tourist excursion and even managed to persuade Edie to go along with them. "Just pretend I'm your guide, relax, and enjoy!" he told them with flourish as they set out.

He explained that tourism was the major industry in Nassau, as well as in all of the Bahamas. Taking them through the public straw market, they saw the fine straw work made from the palmetto fronds which were bleached, dyed, and woven into baskets, bags, and hats. "There are a lot of small industries, too," he pointed out. "Factories for rum, liqueur, paper, textiles, cement, plastics, and rubber goods. The sponge beds are working now, too. A blight hit back in 1939, and it's taken this long to get them going again."

Kelly bought a big, colorful straw hat and teased Edie about not wearing hers any longer. "You're getting to be a real island girl. Look at you—all brown like a native." To Mike, she said, "Back home, you couldn't get her in the sun. She swears it ages a woman quicker than anything."

Edie lifted her chin in a gesture of defiance and spunkily retorted, "Maybe I am going native. And so what if I am? You can't stop the clock from ticking so why not enjoy every second?"

"My kind of gal!" Mike gave her an affectionate pat on the back.

"And another thing," Edie went on with a laugh, pointing to Kelly's newly-purchased hat, "that thing will wind up in your *What-the-heck* closet, anyway, like everything else you buy when you take a trip."

Mike wanted to know what she meant, and Edie explained the closet was a place where she put souvenirs that she'd later look at and ask herself, "*What the heck* did I buy that for?"

"Thank goodness for those closets," he laughed, "because lots of people around here depend on tourist income."

Renting a car, Mike drove them around to show off the shopping areas, theaters, hospital facilities. Then he took them to the Lyford Cay area, on the south shore, where there were multi-million dollar homes, and on to the exclusive Coral Harbour Club development. Then, in a remote area untouched by developers and not likely to be due to the land being owned by those who cherished their privacy, he slowed in front of his own lot and casually remarked, "Now this is where I'd love to build a house one day." He did not reveal it was already his.

"Gorgeous!" Edie exclaimed, gesturing to the wide sweep of pink sand, the glittering turquoise sea beyond. "I can just picture a house here—lots of glass and terraces. Why, you wouldn't even have to landscape. There's already palms and palmettos everywhere."

Mike went on to tell about the coral reef that was visible at low tide. "Makes a perfect channel for a boat. You just have to know exactly where it is."

Kelly chimed in to declare, "It's almost prettier than your Paradise Cove, Mike." Actually, she thought it was even more gorgeous but was afraid it might hurt his feelings to say so.

With a twinkle in his eye, he grinned and pretended to joke, "Well, how about if I buy this place and live here part of the time and call it Paradise *Reef?*"

"Buy the one next to it, while you're at it," she joined in the jest. "Edie and I will build our place there."

At that Edie cried, "Why can't we just all live together? It'd be cheaper."

Kelly let that nuance pass, but Mike was quick to pick up on it. "That sounds like a winner. I'll be busy with my dive shop, and Kelly can go to work for Dr. Brewster, and you can keep house."

Kelly couldn't resist disputing that part of his idea. "Why should I work for Dr. Brewster? I could start my own clinic—a *floating* clinic! I could buy one of those little house boats and make an examination room inside, have portable X-ray equipment, emergency surgical facilities. Then I could have a regular run to the smaller islands and offer vaccinations, inoculations, routine care for the animals there, and . . ." Her voice trailed abruptly as she saw the way they were looking at her. Edie's eyes were glowing, and she had a little know-it-all smirk on her face, like maybe she could see right inside Kelly's heart and know why she was playing along with the dream game, for it wasn't really a game, at all, and she'd actually been thinking of how it might be if she did move to the islands. And Mike was watching her with an expression she could not decipher. Was he thinking maybe she was rushing things to even be joking about such a venture? She gave a self-conscious shrug and terminated the conversation by saying, "Oh, this is silly to even be talking about. Let's go."

They returned to Nassau proper, where Mike ended their day's excursion with a trip to the famous James Bond Bar. Jutting out from a short pier and situated right in the water, it had been the scene of a spectacular water skiing escapade in the filming of *Never Say Never Again*. Edie and Kelly swore the Yellowbirds they drank there were just a tad better than anywhere else they'd sampled them.

On the way back to the island, Edie asked how Kelly's diving lessons were coming along. "Wonderful," Mike assured, beaming proudly at his star student.

"Kelly is a born diver. She's learned quickly and follows instructions to the letter. So far, she hasn't shown any fear." He went on tell how so far they'd only been down among the reefs, but he felt like she'd progressed enough that pretty soon she would be ready to go down to the popular shipwreck site.

Edie glanced at Kelly, as though trying to make her mind up about something, then hesitantly asked, "Well, she tells me she wants to be certified. How long before she succeeds?"

"Well, how much longer will you two be here?" He tried to keep his voice light and not betray the dread he was feeling.

"That's something we've got to talk about soon," she said, more to Kelly than to him.

Again, Mike tried not to give himself away as he pressed, "Have you got any idea? I mean, there are certain requirements. Remember, Kelly?" He wanted to include her in the conversation because she was standing away from them as the boat chugged into Dunmore Town harbor, staring out to sea and apparently lost in her own thoughts.

She was in tune, however, and recited, "Sure, I do, and I still have two sessions of classroom instruction, and I've only had one dive in open water. I've got four to go."

Edie was quiet for a moment, then said, "Well, maybe we'd better think about staying on for a few more weeks."

Kelly and Mike looked at each other the instant she spoke, joy shining on their faces. He wanted to reach out and grab her and hold her tight against him and cover her face with kisses and tell her how happy he was to have that extra time. But he dared not, instead declared, "That's great. A few more weeks is just what we need."

Kelly's heart was pounding, and she wondered just how glad he was that their time together was not going to end as soon as they'd thought. But damnit, she fumed, he was so unreadable. When they made love, it was like they'd been born for each other's arms, absolutely in tune, heart and soul. And when they were alone, diving, or spear-fishing, or just dining out or dancing, doing *anything*, they were totally happy. Yet, nothing serious was ever said about the future.

One afternoon, when he'd gone off by himself, saying he had to take care of some personal business, Kelly had gone down to the Mariner to have lunch and check on Winny and her dog. They were fine, and Anna sat at the table with her since they weren't very busy that day. The conversation had turned to Mike, and Kelly found herself doing something she didn't ordinarily do—prying and probing for information about a man. Yet she was able to easily extricate from Anna that Mike seemingly did have lots of girlfriends. She told herself she shouldn't be surprised. He was probably every girl's idea of what a summer romance should be. The only thing was, with each passing day, she realized she was coming to regard him much more than that, just as she had to face the reality that it could probably never be anything more. She knew him well enough by now to know that marriage would mean living on the islands. Could she do that? Could she give up her world for his? That remained to be seen, but more than that, she had no reason to believe he wanted to marry her. How ironic it all was. Neil had jumped to conclusions, misinterpreting the seriousness of their relationship, wanting to move right along to the altar. Here, Kelly had what she'd thought she wanted all along—no commitments, just fun and sex and don't worry about tomorrow. So why did she feel so disconcerted, so unsure of herself?

She had wanted time to decide exactly how she felt about Neil, whether or not she loved him, and, if so, whether that love might grow and lead her to want to accept his proposal. Now she realized she felt nothing for Neil. He'd been fun to be with, and they'd had good times, in bed and out. But that's all it was, all it ever could be. Mike was partially responsible for that conclusion, for their relationship had personified her negativism over Neil. How could she feel as she did about Mike and be even a little bit in love with anybody else? Maybe some women could, but not her. She was monogamous in affairs of the heart. So she had decided *The Kelly and Neil Show* had run its course. Where did that leave her and Mike? Time was running out. Maybe she should just go home and face the situation. Break it off with Neil, deal with her mother's rage, get an apartment of her own. She and Mike could write to each other, visit back and forth, but damnit, that's not the way she wanted it.

At last, she was torn from her reverie by Edie's admission she was getting a bit tired of the hotel. "If I'd known we'd wind up wanting to stay so long, I'd have tried to find a cottage to rent, where we'd have a place to fix our own meals. Maybe our own little beach."

At that, Mike snapped his fingers. "I know the perfect place." He went on to explain as he steered the boat up to his private pier at the waterfront. "There's this little cottage I look after when the owners aren't here. They don't want to rent it out commercially because it's a real nice place, but they've told me if I know the people, it's okay. We can move you in there as soon as tomorrow, if you like."

"We'd like!" Edie and Kelly cried in unison.

"Then it's settled." He winked at Kelly, blew her a kiss as he stepped up on the pier to secure the boat with lines. "We'll get you all settled first thing in the morning, but it's got to be early. I've got a dive group coming in at ten to go down to the shipwreck. Weatherman calls for rain after lunch, and I want to get down and up before the water gets churned up."

At once, Kelly wanted to know, "Can I go this time? You said I was ready—"

"I said you were *almost* ready," he cut in to correct. "Listen, I don't take anybody down to that site unless they're certified. It's relatively safe, but I have seen sharks down there a few times. Sting rays, too. The only open dive you made was in a place I use strictly for training. I want to do a few more of those before I expose you to possible hazards. I have to be sure you won't panic and do something dangerous like surface too fast and get the bends."

Stiffly, she defended, "I know not to surface faster than my bubbles, and—"

Again, he interrupted, sternly, to remind, "You've had classroom instruction, Kelly, and you've been down in an almost controlled dive area. I'd just feel better if you had a little more experience before I take you down there, okay?"

Edie couldn't resist opining, "With Kelly's track record for being impetuous, I'd sure feel better if you took her slow and easy, Mike."

"Don't worry," he laughed, helping her step up on the dock, then reached for Kelly and made a face at her as she stuck out her tongue at him. "I'm learning how to handle your stubborn granddaughter, believe me."

"That's what *you* think," she fired back but not angrily. She knew only too well he was probably right and would just try harder to prove to him she was competent to make the dive to the shipwreck site.

Mike said he had some things to take care of at the

shop and would see Kelly at the hotel in a little while. She was grateful for the time to take a shower, change, and start some of her packing. Almost every night, she was sleeping with Mike at his place, returning in time to have breakfast with Edie *if* she were around, but more and more lately, she was already up and gone.

Edie was enthused about renting the cottage, and as they walked along in the direction of the hotel said, "It's going to be nice having our place. The Sea Gull is nice, and so are Reeta and the others who work there, it's just that we'll have more privacy, and I like the idea of stocking a refrigerator with things we like."

Kelly felt the need to confirm she intended to pay her part. "You've been whipping out your gold card for everything, and if we're going to stay on awhile longer, you've got to let me help out with expenses."

"You aren't drawing a paycheck right now," Edie pointed out. "Don't worry about it."

"I *do* worry about it because it's not right. Besides, I've been saving quite a bit out of my checks, but I suppose if I don't go back soon, I may not have a job."

"Yes, you will. That's not a problem."

"It might be. I mean, I can't just take an extended leave. They need me at the clinic or they wouldn't have hired me."

Edie felt a little wave of guilt. Still, she wasn't ready yet to confide her influence on Kelly's position at North Side Animal Hospital. Kelly would resent her interference. And maybe she was butting in, anyway, insisting they stay on. Kelly might be ready to go back, though she doubted it. Still, she asked, "I hope I wasn't speaking out of turn back there, saying we'd rent that place and stay on a few more weeks. You *do* want to, don't you?"

Kelly bit her tongue to keep from revealing just *how*

much. "Of course. I'd like to go on and get my certificate. I've come this far. Might as well go all the way."

Edie suspected it was much more than that. "Mike seemed to be very pleased we were staying on. He really likes you, and I wouldn't be surprised if it's getting serious."

"Oh, come on!" Kelly over-rode the tremor within by pretending shock at such a possibility. "He's not the type to get serious about a girl. I mean, he might make a decent living at what he does, but he does it *here*. He's not about to move back to the states to pursue a romance because he doesn't intend to ever live there again. He told me so. This is his world now."

"I didn't say anything about him moving back to the states. Didn't say anything at all about him leaving his world."

"Well, you aren't suggesting I'd leave mine for his?"

"You would if you loved him."

"But *here?*" Kelly gestured wildly, as though she'd never even considered such a thing. "What would I do here? I'm a city girl, and—"

"Kelly, you have always managed to adapt to anything you set your mind to, and you know it. Disregard Mike altogether. If you decided you wanted to make a life here, you would, and you'd adjust and be as happy as you made up your mind to be."

"I think you're the one with island fever. You just want me along for company. Besides . . ." She turned to give her a suspicious glare. "What do you do with yourself all day long, anyway, when I'm off with Mike? We had to practically drag you along with us today. And the evenings? What do you do every evening? You never want to go out to dinner with us."

Edie shrugged, hedged, "I don't like being a fifth

wheel. Young folks have no business feeling obligated to entertain old folks.''

"That's not it, and you know it.''

"Oh, for heaven's sake, Kelly. Stop trying to focus on me to keep from talking about yourself. The truth is, I think you've got yourself even more mixed-up than when we got here.''

"And what is *that* supposed to mean?''

"You wanted time to think things over where Neil is concerned. Have you?''

"I know I don't want to marry him.''

"And Mike?''

Kelly gave up on keeping it a secret. "Okay, you win. Maybe I am having some serious thoughts about what it would be like if I found out I really do love him, and we got married and I settled down here to live. It's scary.''

"Scary?'' Edie stopped walking, turning to stare at her aghast. "For God's sake, what's scary about falling in love and getting married? People do it every day. And don't tell me you're feeling froggy because your first marriage didn't work. That didn't count. You should have just shacked up instead of feeling guilty and wanting to make it legal.''

"Edie!'' Kelly gasped and laughed all at once. "Listen to you!''

"Yes, *do* listen to me!'' she said with a stamp of her foot. "That's one of the few benefits of growing old. You can be as cantankerous and blunt as you want to be, and nobody can do anything about it. It's rude to curse an old lady. So you listen to me, and you listen good because I don't want you to wait till you get my age to realize how stupid you're being.''

"Stupid?'' Kelly echoed. "About what?'' This was a side to Edie she hadn't seen before—defiance, arrogance.

"Love is always a risk, Kelly, because when you take that big step and let yourself fall in love with somebody, they might just reach out and yank your heart right out of your chest and squeeze it till you hurt so bad you want to die. But that's the chance you've got to take because I can't think of anything worse than going through life without daring to love somebody. To hell with the chance you're taking because sometimes you win, and that's worth all the bad times."

Kelly struggled to keep from bursting into delighted laughter because she'd never seen Edie so peppery and adored her for it. "So you are saying I should just let myself go completely, fall in love with Mike, move down here, and be an island girl."

"I'm saying that's what you should do if it's what you want to do. Everything will fall into place. Just don't hold back and be afraid to let your heart lead the way."

"And you'd move down here and live with us?"

"Don't be ridiculous. Not *with* you. Surely you don't take me for one of those grandmother-types who babysit and make homemade cookies? No way! I'd have my own condo and a life of my own, just as I've done since Richard died."

Kelly couldn't resist playfully goading, "Maybe that's the reason you've turned down invitations from all those eager widowers; you're afraid to let go yourself."

"Nonsense. None of them turned me on, that's all."

They looked at each other and burst out laughing, and Kelly was swept with love for her grandmother, promising herself to try to be more like her by facing reality, instead of running from it.

Her first challenge awaited at the hotel. The minute she stepped into her room she saw the flowers. Red roses, white daisies, purple lilies, and lavender orchids, all beautifully arranged amidst greenery and sprigs of delicate white baby's breath. Kelly reached for the card, heart pounding, sure Mike had sent them.

Reeta, passing by, paused at the door to call, "Aren't they lovely? I brought them up myself. The florist in Nassau was so concerned they'd wilt on the boat ride over, that I promised to take special care of them. He says he doesn't get many flower orders from the states."

Edie thanked her to send her on her way and moved to stand next to Kelly as she removed the card from the envelope. Her expression, she noted, was no longer pleased.

"Neil," she said dully, handing her the card for scrutiny. "He misses me."

"Of course, he does," Edie said matter-of-factly. "He wants to marry you, remember? And his only crime was trying too hard."

All at once, Kelly felt a wave of guilt which was not motivated by the flowers. She just knew it was time to stop running, and the first step to taking control of her life was dealing with situations like the one with Neil. "I'll be back in a little while," she said to Edie, who'd walked on into her adjoining room.

"Where are you going? I thought you were going to start packing."

She called over her shoulder, "I'll do that when I get back. Right now, I'm going to do what you told me to start doing—face reality. I'm calling Neil to tell him I'm never going to marry him."

Edie stepped to the door to stare after her in wonder. By golly, she thought with a triumphant grin, maybe the babies weren't mixed up in the hospital all those years ago, as she'd jokingly accused when Walter turned out to be such a wimp. Kelly just might turn out to have her genes, after all!

TEN

Kelly was disappointed Neil was not at home when she telephoned; she'd psyched herself up for the confrontation. Worse, his mother had answered the phone, squealing in delight, "Kelly, darling, how wonderful to hear your voice. How are you doing? When are you coming home? I guess I don't have to tell you Neil is beside himself. He misses you so terribly. He didn't know where to write, but your mother tracked you down, it seems. And poor Verna! She's a basket case with you gone."

So what else is new, Kelly had felt like asking. Instead, she skirted Dodie's questions with one of her own, "When will he be back? I can call him later."

"Oh, there's no telling," she had cooed. "He's been taking diving lessons with the kids at the Y, and then they go out for pizza. You know how they are," she had giggled.

Kelly had softly groaned. *Kids!* Dodie always referred to Larry and Brenda and Chad and Vickie as *kids*. She probably thought they went to *Showbiz Pizza* and ate while watching the puppet show. And how ironic it was that she'd never found time to take diving lessons with the others and here she was plunging headfirst into the water and also into love, it seemed. Finally, she had said, "Well, tell him I'll call him tomorrow."

"I can have him call you when he gets in. What's the number there, dear?"

"Never mind. Nice talking to you, Dodie. Bye."

When she had returned to the hotel, Mike was there waiting on the porch. Edie was keeping him company, and Kelly answered the question in her eyes with a slight shake of her head to let her know she hadn't been able to reach Neil.

Mike had brought his Jeep and he and Kelly headed to the cove for a swim.

Kelly couldn't help herself. The dread of knowing she had to talk to Neil was like a pall on the evening. Mike sensed something was bothering her, and, hoping to get her mind off whatever it was, suggested they go out for the evening. She was all for it. He took her to an island bar where there was a steel drum band for entertainment and dancing. They both got in the spirit of things, doing the limbo, trying the *Lambada*. Anna was there and eagerly introduced Kelly to her fiance, and she found herself making new friends. They were invited to a cookout on Saturday night, and another couple wanted them to go into Nassau for an evening of nightclub and barhopping. Others suggested future outings like an open dive, once Kelly got her certificate, and one young man had a deep sea boat and said they had to all get together for an all-day outing soon. Depression and apprehension faded along with the night. The bar closed at three A.M., and Kelly and Mike found themselves included in a raid on the Mariner's kitchen, led by Anna. When they finally stepped outside, darkness was being assaulted by the first creeping fingers of dawn on the eastern horizon. Mike groaned,

"Oh, no. Where'd the night go?" He glanced at his watch. "I've got time for about three hours sleep before moving you all to the cottage and then taking that group out to the shipwreck."

Kelly gave an exaggerated sigh of frustration, said, "Well, I guess I'll take pity on you and excuse you from a torrid lovemaking session."

"Hey, you're not exactly the image of desire right now yourself," he bantered right back. "How about if we recharge our batteries, and I'll be by to get you and Edie and your luggage around eight o'clock?"

Kelly was as exhausted as he was for sleep, but when he pulled the Jeep up in front of the hotel, the fires ignited when they kissed in parting. "Tonight," he warned in a husky voice as he gently cupped her breasts, "you're going to beg for mercy."

Reaching to dance her fingertips along his thigh, she brazenly whispered, "Oh, yeah? We'll see who begs!"

He gave her a gentle push and a mock growl, "Get out of here, before I throw you in the back and take you here and now, woman!"

"Promises, promises!" She laughed, scurrying out of the Jeep and skipping happily up the walkway to disappear inside after throwing him a quick kiss from the doorway.

Tip-toeing, Kelly made her way upstairs. She was just about to unlock her door when it opened abruptly, and she found herself staring up into Edie's sleepy and agitated face.

"It's been one hell of a night!" she said, almost accusingly, then rushed on to irritably tell her, "Neil must be drunk! He got the number here, and he's been calling all night long."

Kelly rushed inside to close the door after her. "But why? Didn't you just tell him I'd call him back?"

"Believe me, I tried. Reeta woke me up about mid-

night, said there was a long distance call for you. I
went down to the desk to see who it was, and when I
answered and found out it was Neil, naturally, he
wanted to know where you were at such an hour. I told
him you were out with *girl*friends, and I'd tell you he
called.

"Well," she gave a disgusted sigh, plopping down
wearily in a chair beside the bed before continuing, "he
called again an hour later. Reeta had gone to bed, but
the phone rings in her room because business isn't brisk
enough to keep a desk clerk on duty all night. She let
me know that, by the way, when she had to come up
here again. I told her to tell him you weren't in yet,
so he called back again at three A.M., and by then
Reeta was really getting annoyed, so I went to talk to
him and asked him to please stop calling. He got real
upset then and wanted to know just what kind of *girl*-
friends you'd taken up with that stayed out all night."

Kelly was shaking her head slowly from side to side
in disgust and disbelief. He had to have been drunk.

"So I got mad and hung up on him. The next time
he called, Reeta did the same thing, but she came up
here to wake me up and let me know she had."

"I don't guess she'll be disappointed to find out
we're moving out this morning."

"No. I told her that to try to smooth things over,
and I think it made her whole night. So I guess you'd
better call him and get it over with, before he calls and
wakes her up again. It's been about an hour since the
last one."

"He's probably passed out by now."

"Don't count on it. To be honest, he sounded more
mad than drunk."

They looked at each other as from far, far away came
the sound of a telephone ringing. Doggedly, Kelly
headed for the door, was halfway down the stairs when

Reeta appeared at the bottom, robe wrapped around her, weary-eyed from lack of sleep.

"Please! Talk to him! Because after this, I am taking the phone off the hook." She pointed to the phone on the desk. "Take it there." Scowling, she stormed out, and Kelly heard her door slam in finality.

Kelly took a deep breath, lifted the receiver, and demanded, "Neil, are you out of your mind? You've kept everyone here up all night, and—"

"What I want to know," he exploded at once, voice crackling across the wires, "is what *you* were doing out all night? What kind of people are you hanging around with down there in the middle of nowhere?"

Not about to lose control, she very coolly told him, "Where I was, and who I was with, is none of your business, Neil."

"Hey," came a snarling retort, "*you* called *me*, remember? I thought maybe there was an emergency."

"I told Dodie I'd call you back. I did not leave word for you to return my call, and when you called the first time, Edie told you I'd get back to you. But you kept on calling because you were checking up on me, and I don't like that. Besides . . ." She decided to plunge ahead, get right to the point of why she'd called him in the first place, "I only called you to say thanks for the flowers, but you shouldn't have. I've decided that even though you're a nice guy, and I like you a lot, and we had some great times together, there's just not enough there to build a future on, and—"

"What the hell are you trying to tell me?" he screamed then, rage boiling over. "Kelly, I want to know—what the hell are you saying here? That it's all over?"

"No," she said with the simple tone one used with a child, "I'm saying it never began. I *didn't* love you, *don't* love you, *can't* love you. There's no karma. I'm sorry, but that's the way it is. I don't want to hurt you, but—''

"Hurt *me?*" he yelped. "Hurt *me,* did you say? Listen, Kelly, I'm hurting, all right, but it's nothing compared to what you're doing to yourself. I don't know what's going on down there, but you're all mixed up. You don't know what you're doing. We had a great thing going, and we're perfect for each other, and you know it. Granted, maybe I rushed you a little bit. Your mother told me how you have to be coddled along because you've always been rebellious, so I should've given you more time. I'm willing to do that. We can be engaged to *be* engaged, for God's sake, but you've got to come back home, right now, so we can start working on it.

"And your mother!" He went on after a dramatic sigh, "That poor woman! She's headed for a nervous breakdown. She loves you so much, and she's worried sick about your being off down there with Edie because Edie's getting senile, and—"

At that, Kelly blew. "Edie is *not* senile! She's just about the most level-headed person I've ever met, and if my mother had half the common sense she's got, we wouldn't have been at war with each other all these years.

"Now you get something straight once and for all, and you can pass the message along to my folks. I'm staying down here till I get good and ready to come back, and that's the way it is. I'm a big girl now, and I don't need you or anybody else telling me how to live my life."

"Kelly, wait! Don't be mad." He was afraid she was going to hang up. "I love you, and I want to marry you. We're perfect for each other and—"

"You only *think* you love me because our families have pushed us together and convinced you we're meant for each other. For the last time, I don't want to hurt you, but I'm not going to be manipulated by you or anybody else." *God, it felt good,* she realized, *to just let it all out instead of beating around the bush or running from reality.*

Anger returning because he wasn't getting anywhere begging, he lashed out again, "You'll come to your senses, Kelly, because you know we're perfect for each other. Now I want you to come home and get away from the influence of your crazy grandmother, and—"

Kelly hung up. She'd had it. To hell with him, to hell with her parents.

She walked out on the porch to gaze out at the peach and golden sunrise. There, in the tranquility of a new day dawning, Kelly knew she wasn't going back home any time soon. Now there were more questions to be answered, more problems to be solved than ever before. Did she truly love Mike or was he a part of the eternal rebellion within? She needed time to find out, and by God, she was going to have it. No matter the consequences.

Hurrying back upstairs, she found Edie waiting to hear what had been said. After she recounted the conversation, Kelly tersely declared, "I do want to stay on here for awhile, but I think it's only fair for me to call Dr. Zealy and tell him to be looking for a replacement because when I do go back, I think I'd be happier leaving Charlotte. It was stupid of me to think I could ever get along with Mom and Dad, that we could be like a real family."

Edie shook her head in pity. "It's a shame. Life is so short for things to have to be this way. I know you wanted to settle down, have peace, and it would've been nice if you and Neil had been meant for each other."

Kelly had to agree with that. "There's nothing wrong

with Neil. It's just that something is missing there, and as long as I feel that way, I won't marry him or anybody else.''

"Good for you!" Edie got up to give her a big hug. "Now let's get some sleep. Today's going to be really exciting. After we get our things over to the cottage, we'll ask Captain Grady to let us ride with him into Nassau so we can go to a big grocery store there and buy lots of junk food for our kitchen!''

Kelly did lie down, but sleep didn't want to come. Her brain was whirling. Mike had said she could go with him on the shipwreck dive, but only for the ride. He absolutely refused to let her go below with everyone else. But, instead, she decided to go into Nassau as Edie wanted. Something told her she needed to do some looking around on her own, be alone with her thoughts for a time.

Finally, she dozed, but all too soon it was time to get up and get ready to move out of the hotel. Mike arrived promptly at eight. He drove them and their luggage over to the cottage, and they fell in love with it on sight.

"A screened porch with an ocean view!" Edie happily cried. "And both bedrooms are on the front to catch the breeze.''

Mike, standing beside Kelly, slipped his arms around her waist and nuzzled the back of her neck as he whispered, "As if I intend to let you spend much time in *your* bedroom. I much prefer mine.''

Edie had gone to explore the kitchen, and Kelly turned to welcome his kiss, reveling in the splendor before telling him she'd decided not to go with him.

"Sure," he said, hiding his disappointment in his continued endeavor to give her free rein in all decisions, not about to coax her into going with him if she didn't want to. "I'll just come by later, okay?''

"Okay," she responded absently, wishing he'd act like he really minded that she wasn't going. That little niggling feeling was starting up again that made her wonder and want to find out just how much she did mean to him.

Kelly was only slightly surprised that Edie and Captain Grady seemed like old friends as they started out across the inlet to Nassau. She'd probably seen him around during her frequent walks on the beach and waterfront. She sat beside him at the helm, and they chatted animatedly, obviously enjoying each other's company. They'd make a wonderful couple, Kelly mused, when, and if, Edie decided she could open her heart to love again. How she wished that would happen. Edie just didn't fit into the role society decreed for little old ladies and widows. Decked out in blue jeans or whatever outfit caught her fancy, she wasted no time in front of a TV set watching soap operas and living life vicariously. The only problem was, however, her friends *did* adhere to what society expected, so she had no one in her age group to share her interests.

Onshore, Kelly was about to ask Edie if she would mind finding something to do with herself for a few hours, when Captain Grady shyly asked if she'd like to join them for lunch. She merrily declined, said she had wanted to stop by Dr. Brewster's clinic and took off in that direction.

He was quite busy, as usual, but took time to say hello and ask if she would like to hang around for awhile, which she did. "I wish I could put you on my staff," Dr. Brewster said more than once. "Any time you want a job, you've got one."

He persuaded her to assist in surgery, and she did so, monitoring anesthesia, knowing which instruments to hand him without his asking, stepping in to close and suture. Without realizing it, several hours whizzed by, and then the receptionist came back to where Kelly was setting up an IV to let her know some people were out front asking for her.

"We just wanted to know if you were ready to go back to the island," Edie said when Kelly came out, wearing a soiled lab coat and looking very at home there. "But we can see you're busy."

She assured she was, adding, "I can catch a ride over later. Boats are always coming and going. You two go on back. They're really busy here, and I didn't have anything else to do with Mike on a dive."

Captain Grady was quick to say, "Oh, we're in no hurry. There's a movie playing I've been wanting to see." He glanced at his watch. "How about if you meet us at the dock in, say, two hours? Will you be ready by then?"

"I hope so," Dr. Brewster interjected with a laugh as he overheard in passing. "If not, we're all going to pass out from weariness."

And, almost two hours later, he was thanking Kelly for making his wish come true. "You've been a God-send. Here." He handed her several bills. "A hundred dollars. It's worth more, but—"

"No!" she quickly declined. "I didn't do it for the money. I just missed working. But if you don't mind, I would like to use your phone to call my boss back in the states."

He said of course and offered her use of his private office. She made the call and caught Dr. Zealy just as he was about to leave for the day. Explaining she wanted to extend her leave of absence, he told her to go right ahead, saying things were slow, not to worry, have a good time.

Taking a cab to the waterfront, she arrived about twenty minutes early. She browsed in the nearby straw market for a little while, then, returning to the pier, was thrilled to spot Mike's boat. He was nowhere in sight, but she knew he had to be close by. When Edie and Captain Grady arrived, she'd tell them she'd go back with him instead.

She started towards his boat—then froze.

Mike was coming up from the bottom of the boat, but he was not alone. A very pretty girl in a white bikini with long black hair streaming down her back was with him. He walked across the deck with her, and, just as she was about to step up on the pier, Kelly's eyes bugged out as she threw her arms around his neck, pressed her near-naked body against his and give him what looked like a very passionate kiss.

Stunned, infuriated, washed with instinctive jealousy, Kelly turned away, did not see how Mike abruptly pushed the girl away before she could really get into the kiss, did not see the way she laughed, gave a carefree toss of her long hair, and went nonchalantly on her way.

Mike had turned away, then happened to see Kelly and was right behind her, calling to her, but she kept on going, blinded by her tears. Finally catching up to whirl her around and meet his searching gaze, he demanded, "Hey, what's this all about?"

"*Hey!*" she mocked, pointing towards his boat. "What was all *that* about?" But then, indignity and anger melted into humiliation, and she quickly shook her head and said, "I'm sorry. It's none of my business. I don't own you, and—"

She tried to turn away, lest he see the tears welling in her eyes, but he held tight, gave her a gentle shake. The play of a smile was on his lips. "If you saw all that back there, then you know *she* kissed *me*, and if you'd kept on watching, you'd have seen me push her away."

She forced a casual shrug. "You don't owe me an explanation, really."

"Yes, I do, because you can believe if I see some guy kissing you, I'll want to know what's going on. That girl lives here in Nassau. Her father owns one of the big hotels. We went together for awhile when I first came down here, but it didn't work out. We're still friends. She books a dive group once in awhile, and when she does, she tries to get something going again. She's a spoiled, rich brat used to getting her way and doesn't give up easily. But that's her problem, not mine, because she doesn't mean a damn thing to me."

Kelly had been surprised by the intensity of her own relief, struggled within to pretend nonchalance. "Like I said, it's your business, and you don't owe me any explanation. I had no right to say anything, and—"

"Damnit, Kelly!" He gripped her shoulders and shook her harder. All of a sudden he knew he'd had it. All afternoon, he'd missed her like hell. It had been hard to concentrate on what he was doing because he wasn't doing it *with her*. No matter he'd promised himself to play it cool, it was time she realized things were getting serious, at least on his part. Searching her face, desperately seeking some sign that she was feeling the same way about him, he told her, almost angrily, "Don't you realize I don't *want* another woman?"

Kelly's heart began to pound with the realization that he *did* care! "But you never said anything—"

"Maybe I was waiting for you to make the first move."

"Oh, Mike," she melted against him then, confessing, "I don't want anybody else, either. All I want is time for us to see where all this is going to take us."

"As long as you're honest with me about how you feel, as long as you're honest with me about everything,

I'll give you all the time you need, Kelly. I promise that."

They sealed their newfound awareness with a deep and stirring kiss, parting only when Edie hesitantly tapped Kelly on the shoulder and said in a voice mimicking her mother, "Really, Kelly, young ladies of culture and refinement don't conduct themselves like this in public."

Laughing, they drew apart. "I guess I won't be going back with you and Captain Grady," Kelly told her, reveling in the way Mike caught her hand to possessively squeeze.

Edie pretended to give him a scathing look and snapped, "Well, you watch out for this one. He looks like a rogue to me."

"He is!" Kelly cried, as he lifted her up and tossed her over his shoulder like a pirate carrying off his booty. "And I'm loving every minute of it!"

Edie was still watching after them when Burt stepped up beside her to whisper in her ear, "I'd carry *you* off like that, if I didn't know I'd wind up in bed on a heating pad."

She turned to flash him an adoring look, felt a warm rush at just his nearness. Never had she dreamed she could ever feel this way about a man again. With a wink, she pluckily told him, "Well, I don't want you straining yourself, sailor, 'cause I can sure think of lots more things for you to do in bed besides lie on a heating pad!"

ELEVEN

Kelly was delighted that Edie was interested in Burt Grady. She absolutely glowed, looked twenty years younger. No doubt, the secret romance had been going on since they'd first arrived, and she couldn't wait to see where it went. But, like her own involvement with Mike, only time would tell.

Just three days after they'd moved out of the hotel and into the cottage, Kelly was excitedly waiting for Mike to come by, as he'd said he felt she was ready to dive with him to the shipwreck. Keeping an eye out the window, expecting him to pull up any second on his Moped, she was puzzled when Reeta came bustling up on the path and onto the porch. She spoke briefly with Edie, then left.

"So what was all that about?" she wanted to know when she went outside.

With a sigh of resignation because she'd been expecting something like it, Edie revealed, "It seems Verna is trying to get in touch with us to let us know Walter is very ill. She claims he's having heart problems."

Kelly likewise knew it was probably a maneuver to

get her to go home but nonetheless felt a stab of apprehension. "So what do we do? We can't ignore it."

"I don't intend to. You go ahead with your plans for the day, and I'll walk down to the telephone office and call Walter's doctor and find out for myself. I'm sure it's another of Verna's attempts at emotional blackmail."

Kelly knew she wouldn't relax till they were sure. "Would you mind calling now? I'll go with you."

Edie obliged, and they went together. It did not take long to find out from the doctor, that, so far as he knew, Walter wasn't having any problems. In fact, he hadn't seen him since his last check-up, nearly six months ago. He even went so far as to say he doubted Walter would've changed doctors because he'd have known if there'd been a request for transferal of records. Edie, embarrassed over the situation, apologized for having bothered him and hung up. To Kelly, she said, "It wouldn't have done any good to tell him how your mother is. He isn't her doctor, and he'd never believe it!

"Now," she urged, "you go on and have fun. I think it's time I called her and straightened her out about a thing or two."

"Nobody ever straightens her out," Kelly cynically reminded. "She does what she wants to do. Always has. Always will."

"Maybe that's true, but this time, she's gone too far. I don't appreciate her playing 'Wolf.' It's just not right, and I'm going to let her know it. Then I'm calling Walter at the drugstore and let him know what she's done."

"Then what? She'll have a super attack, for sure, land in the hospital again and blame you and me."

Edie laughed. "Do I look like I care? Don't worry about it dear. We're not going home till we're good and ready, and I'm going to let her know she's just wasting her time with her schemes."

Kelly decided she didn't want to hang around for the explosion and took off to meet Mike. It was days like this that made her all the more determined to stay forever!

He explained he'd feel more comfortable about her going along if she wore a rubber diving suit, explaining, "When you dive in water that's anything less than normal body temperature, the water conducts heat directly away from the body surface in direct proportion to the difference in temperatures between your body and the water."

"But it's summer time," she reminded. "Will the water actually be *that* cold?"

"Even in warm weather months here, the bottom layers of water can be as much as thirty degrees colder than the surface layers, but as you get more dive experience, you won't need to wear a suit here in the Bahamas. I just don't want you to get down there and start shivering, because you'll use up all your energy, and you won't be enjoying yourself like you should."

In an open dive, Mike always left someone onboard to be prepared to assist if needed, as well as keep an eye on the line and floating marker that indicated divers were below. Since just he and Kelly were going down, he hired Anna's cousin, Ronnie, an experienced diver himself, for the outing.

Once below, Kelly was fascinated with the sight of the wreck of a frigate, established sometime between the late 18th or early 19th century. Mike used sign-language to point out unmistakable outlines of muzzle-loading cannon, indentifiable even through the growth of coral.

There was so much to see and explore, and time passed all too quickly and soon Mike was giving the signal it was time for them to surface. No matter that they had plenty of air left in their tanks, one of the things he'd stressed in classroom instruction was that staying down long beyond depths of thirty-three feet, a diver can become drunk from the nitrogen in the tank. The bloodstream could absorb air under pressure, causing crippling air bubbles to form on returning to the surface.

As they began their ascent, no faster than their smallest bubbles, they held hands. Through his mask, Kelly could see the desire in his eyes, knew her own was probably likewise mirrored for him to see. He reached out to touch her breast, and she was surprised to feel the heated sensation even through the dive suit. He was likewise wearing one, so she wouldn't feel quite as weird, and she boldly reached to touch him intimately. He wagged a no-no sign with his finger. The suit fit like a second skin. There was no room for an erection! She wanted to laugh, which was impossible with her mouthpiece, and he pounded his fists together with a mock menacing glare to warn she'd pay later.

When, at last, they were back onboard, Kelly stripped out of her suit, down to the bikini she wore beneath, lifted her face to the blistering sun above and drank in the pungent salt air and jubilantly declared, "Harbour Island, the Bahamas! I could stay forever!"

And Mike silently urged, *Do it!*

Edie later related her conversation with Verna, admitting it wasn't as she'd expected. "She wasn't angry. She actually apologized for upsetting me, said she never meant to but she was just concerned about Walter being so depressed over your not coming home. She wanted to know what we were doing that was so important, and I told her we'd found paradise and weren't ready to leave it quite yet."

"And?" Kelly prodded apprehensively. "What happened then?"

Edie snickered "Do you have to ask? She started crying, of course, said her heart was broken, and if you didn't come back, she hoped she died. You should know the routine by now."

Kelly did, but it didn't make it any easier, and, right then, she couldn't bring herself to approach the subject of moving to the island on a trial basis. It just didn't seem like the right time.

A few days later, Mike had a free day with no dives scheduled, so he asked Anna to prepare and pack a picnic lunch in waterproof bags. Kelly was thrilled to discover she was, at last, going to the underwater cave. They drove in his Jeep to a remote section of beach where there were several large formations of coral and sandstone.

"What we're going to do," he explained as they readied their gear, put on their flippers, "is swim under the rock formation over there. We have to go down about twenty feet, and I'll lead the way to a small tunnel through the rock. It comes out in an underwater pool inside that formation."

Kelly held up a hand in feigned protest. "Wait! I can't go! Not yet. If it's as beautiful as you say it is, I want to go back and get everything I'll need to stay at least a week."

Humoring her, he grinned, "Don't worry. The formation forms a ring around the pool. We can have food and water dropped from helicopters, along with furniture for the cave when we decide how you want to decorate."

Laughing, hand in hand, they backed into the water. Soon, they were deep enough to swim, at last reaching beyond where the breakers began to roll in. Before adjusting his mask and inserting his air tube, Mike instructed, "Just stick close behind me. It'll be about a five minute swim."

He dove down, with Kelly following as she tried to ignore the brilliant schools of fish darting around, the dazzling coral and colorful seashells on the sandy bottom. When at last they surfaced, she at once spit out her air tube and cried, "Oh, my God, Mike! It's like something out of a fairy tale."

They were, indeed, in a cave with walls that shimmered in shades of rose and gold and silver. The air was sweet and clean, and as they swam out and into the open pool, she saw that sand had washed up to make a delicate beach area.

They removed their tanks and flippers and went exploring. The cave, itself, was not very large, and they didn't venture far in for fear of drop-offs or other unknown perils. Kelly marveled at the splendor, swore she could live there if need be. He told her there was an island in the Caribbean where a couple did live in a house built out of a cave. "It's fitted to a cliff beneath a vault of rock, with thirteen free-formed rooms. They had an architect build around the natural rock formation, and they live there year-round. I saw it once, from a ship. It's really something."

"That's called really getting away from it all. It would take some getting used to, but I suppose anything is possible."

"I wonder what it would be like—the two of us living here together. Would we get *cave* fever, you think?"

They were walking back towards the little beach, hand in hand and struck with awe by the sheer reverence of their surroundings. Kelly spoke without really thinking of how she was bearing her heart and soul,

"I think we'd be happy together anywhere, Mike. I don't think we'd need anything but each other."

He stopped walking, turned to take her in his arms, blue eyes searching her face to ultimately discover the sincerity he'd hoped for. "You mean that, don't you?"

She could only nod with temerity, for she'd gone too far to offer a quip or light response. "I do, Mike," she whispered then, melding into his embrace. "I've never been so happy with anyone my whole life."

"And I feel the same." He gazed down at her adoringly, brushing her wet hair back from her face as he showered her with tiny, happy kisses. "I've never met anyone like you, Kelly. You make me glad just to be alive. I wonder now how I survived before you came into my world."

"*Your world* . . ." she mouthed the words in wonder, for there was explicit meaning there, and they both knew it. "*Your world* would have to be mine, wouldn't it?"

A grimness descended. "There's no place for me in yours, and frankly, I don't think you've got it so good there, yourself. That's why you came here, anyway, isn't it? To get yourself together to cope with the problems back there?"

"Yes, but instead, I've found a reason to stay here."

Overcome with emotion and desire to consummate their new awareness, he moved to claim her lips in a searing kiss. When at last he released her, he cried, "Kelly, you don't know how much you mean to me . . ."

"Show me!" she commanded then, quickly stripping out of her bikini. "Show me exactly how much."

His hands moved down her back to cup her firm buttocks and press her against him. Lifting her slightly so that she stood on tiptoe, his erect shaft slid between her thighs, and she trembled deliciously as he touched the special place that sent sweet-hot fire dancing through her loins.

Gently he lowered her to the sand, easing his body down upon her. His mouth continued to crush against hers as she opened her legs to him, thrusting her buttocks upward to meet his first thrusts into the velvet recesses of her body. And she received him, all of him, marveling that her own body could accept such a magnificently built man. Her legs wrapped around his back to hold him even closer, wanting everything he had to give. She reveled in his embrace and wanted this hour, this time, to continue for all eternity, as relentlessly and unendingly as the foaming breakers crashing on the shore beyond.

"Kelly, oh, Kelly, you're all I ever want," he murmured, raising his mouth so his lips barely touched hers, though his tongue moved to and fro, flicking at hers to tease her into a frenzy as his manhood pushed in and out.

She felt the crescendo building from within the confines of her belly, and Mike felt it also, and he drove even harder into her. Her lips parted in a scream of ecstacy that echoed and resounded along the rainbow hued walls about them. Wave after wave of passion shuddered through her body, and then he was crying outloud in his own glory as he ground mercilessly into her, driving her buttocks into the rough sand and filling her with his seed.

Afterwards, they lay still, quiet, for long moments as each was lost in the wake of emotions almost frightening in intensity. At last, Mike knew he had to say what he was feeling. Raising up on one elbow so he could look down into her passion-warmed eyes, he began, "In case you don't already know it, I'm in love with you. I think from day one, I knew I wanted it to last, but it's like I told you, I've been burned before when I let it be known I'm not leaving here.

"Understand, Kelly," he continued after a pause to allow her to grasp everything he sought to convey, "that I'm not trying to be selfish or macho, expecting you to give up your world for mine. All I can offer you is love and the sharing of the paradise I've found here. If that's not what you want, if you can't find the happiness here that I've found, I'll understand, because no matter how much I care about you, I'm not going to try to persuade you to do anything you don't want to do."

"You can't be more honest than that," she smiled up at him, adoring him.

"I just don't want any more complications in my life. I promised myself if I could help it, I'd never get caught up in a stressful situation again, and that includes love. I know you've got some problems back home with your folks, and I'll help any way I can. I'm just glad there's nothing else, like a jealous lover. It's a relief to know I'm not competing with anybody for your heart, and the only thing I've got to worry about is whether you can truly be happy here."

For an instant, Kelly felt a twinge of guilt but told herself once more there was no need to explain anything about Neil.

He sensed her tension, raised an eyebrow and asked, "Is something wrong? If you've got reservations, doubts, questions, let's talk about it."

Pushing aside memories of the past, she took a positive note. "I think it can all be worked out. What I'd like to do is talk to Edie, see how she feels about staying on with me. She doesn't have anything to hold her in North Carolina. She might even be getting serious about Captain Grady."

"If she is, there's nothing to worry about. He's a

fine man. I met him when I first came down here. He'd already been here a few years himself. He'd lived in Minnesota his whole life, and when his wife died after they'd been married over forty years, he was being eaten alive with loneliness. Everywhere he turned, he said, he was slapped in the face with memories of how happy they were, all the good times. They'd never had children, so he had no family, no reason to stay. He bought a boat, came down here, made the sea his mistress, as the saying goes. But now, who knows? Maybe you're going to get a new grandfather.''

"As long as he makes her happy, it's fine with me. One thing for sure, though, I want to go to work. As much fun as we have together, I have to admit I'm getting a little bit restless wanting to get back into veterinary medicine. If Dr. Brewster will hire me just part-time, while I give this new life a try, I'll feel like I'm doing something worthwhile *and* helping out with expenses. If Edie does decide to stay, too, then we'll need to find something to rent so we don't have to worry about the owners coming in and wanting to use their place.''

"You don't have to worry about that. They only come down in the winter months, and this is June. By then, who knows? You might have someplace else to live, anyway, on a permanent basis.'' That was as close as he dared come for the time being in letting her know marriage was his ultimate goal if all else worked out.

His fingers trailed down her arm, and he knew if they stayed where they were, with her lying naked in his arms, no matter they'd just made wild, passionate love—he'd take her again. "We'd better eat lunch now. We've got to have time for the food to settle before we start the swim back.'' Already it was after twelve.

Anna had packed ham and cheese sandwiches and brownies with coconut frosting. There was also a small jug of lemonade. They ate their fill, then went for another walk. Kelly could not resist collecting a few shells to take back for souvenirs. She saw a particularly pretty one. Reddish orange in color, it appeared to be covered in black lace, but as she reached for it, Mike quickly knocked her hand away. "Don't touch it. It's poison."

Curious, she knelt beside him as he explained. "It's a *Cone* shell. They're found all over the world, and because they *are* so pretty, people are always getting bitten. You see, there's a little creature inside, and if you pick it up by the snout, he's got a little tooth that shoots out and penetrates with venom. Depending on the individual's reaction, it causes pain, paralysis, or death.

"I've gone over the basic things to watch out for in the water," he continued, "but I've got a book back at the shop you need to read and memorize. There's all kinds of things to watch out for in the water. For instance, we have warm waters here, and lots of fire coral that can cause a painful sting. One brush against that, and you know where it gets its name."

They found a comfortable spot on the beach, where a cool breeze wafted from above. Kelly lay with her head on Mike's chest. They were lost in each other as they talked of any and everything, but then the smoldering ashes of passion began to ignite into renewed flames of desire, and they made love again . . . but not quite as intensely. It was solemn, almost reverent, as though to celebrate their newly avowed love and their intent to go forward together to discover whether it was the real and lasting kind that tomorrows and forever are made of.

That night, they were invited to a cook-out being given by friends of Mike's who lived on Eleuthera.

Though they could have driven the Jeep along the natural but narrow connecting causeway, they opted for the boat instead. More and more lately, they'd been anchoring in the cove to sleep onboard. Kelly loved the gentle bobbing of the craft in the undulating waves. She also enjoyed having fresh-brewed coffee on deck and watching the glorious sunrise.

Kelly had met just about everyone attending. Anna was there, too, and when Mike confided about Kelly giving serious thought to staying on, taking a job with Dr. Brewster, she led a toast to celebrate. "See how popular you are already?" he pointed out, then teased, "But beware. They might expect you to treat their animals for free."

"Don't forget my mother says I'm crazy because I'm a pushover for charity cases."

He was quick to dispute that. "I don't think that's crazy at all. It's called having a heart, and that's nothing to apologize for."

After the party, they cruised back at a leisurely pace, arms about each other as they stood in dreamy silence at the bow. By the time Mike dropped anchor in the cove, they were both almost trembling with desire to taste once more the glory of their passion.

The next morning, they were again awakened by sunlight streaming through the porthole, realized they'd overslept.

Mike groaned, "I've got a dive group coming in from Nassau at nine. We'd better just head on to my pier."

When they arrived, Kelly said she needed to change clothes, would meet him back at the boat within an hour. He told her just to take the Jeep, but she opted for his Moped. Finally heading down the sandy path, she saw that Edie wasn't on the porch with her morning coffee, smiled to think maybe she, too, had stayed out all night. Yet, as she parked the bike, glancing up at the cottage, it was obvious Edie was around. The front door was open, as were all the windows.

Skipping merrily up the steps, she called, "Arise and shine, sleepy-head. I've got time for one cup of java with you, and—"

She froze at the sight of her mother pushing open the screen door to step onto the porch. Though she was smiling in greeting, her eyes were cold, calculating.

She held up a mug. "How about coffee with your mother instead? I've missed you so much, Kelly Jean."

TWELVE

"When . . . when did you get here?" Kelly stammered as she managed to make her way on up the steps. Verna was waiting to give her a hug, shower her face with kisses. Beyond her, Kelly could see Edie watching from the doorway, shaking her head in a gesture of helplessness.

"My flight got in late yesterday." Verna made her tone bright, cheery, as she at last ended her embrace and walked over to sit down in one of the porch chairs. "I wanted to surprise you, so I chartered a boat to bring me here, to Harbour Island, but when I got to the Sea Gull hotel, where you told me you were staying, they said you'd checked out. I really panicked then but thought, *hoped* . . ." she paused for effect, "that you were actually on your way home. Then they told me you'd rented this . . . this place . . ." She lifted her hand to gesture, wrinkled her nose in scorn.

Just then, Edie came out, offering Kelly a sympathetic look along with a mug of steaming coffee.

Verna airily continued, "I had no idea you two had set up housekeeping, for goodness sake. When were you going to let us know you weren't planning on coming home any time soon? And really, dear, don't you think Dr. Zealy at least deserves some consideration? I mean, you can't just take an extended vacation, Kelly. He has a clinic to run, and—''

"I called Dr. Zealy,'' Kelly interrupted her tirade to inform. "I asked if he minded if I stayed on awhile, and he told me not to worry, that things are slow right now. He didn't seem to mind, at all.''

Verna blinked her eyes rapidly, as though totally baffled and bewildered. "But why didn't you call *me*, dear, and let me know your plans? Don't you think that was terribly inconsiderate? After all, you ran away when I was in the hospital at death's door, and that was cruel enough without your just staying away with no explanation.'' She shot a condemning glare at Edie. "Granted, you were being influenced by someone else, but I thought I deserved better treatment than this from you, after all I've done for you. Do I need to remind you how I almost died giving birth to you?''

"No, you don't,'' Kelly was quick to assure, "and it's unfair of you to blame Edie for anything, and I think you're forgetting that when I *did* call you, you got hysterical, and I couldn't talk to you.''

Airily, she laughed. "Well, of course, I did. You hurt me terribly, Kelly, taking off like that. Don't you know that I love you, and your father loves you, and the only thing we've got to live for now is you?'' She leaned forward, holding out her hands in a gesture of pleading, tears welling in her eyes. "When you decided to move back home after you graduated, don't you remember how happy that made me? Why, I spent a fortune redecorating that apartment over the garage so you'd be comfortable there and have some privacy. I had my little girl back! It made me cry for joy to think how wonderful it was going to be for all of us to be together at Christmas, Thanksgiving, birthdays. I even dared think ahead to how it'd be when you got married one day and settled down nearby. I'd have grandchildren to love and play with, bake cookies for.''

Edie rolled her eyes. The closest her daughter-in-law had ever come to making homemade cookies was slicing a roll of refrigerated dough bought in a grocery store dairy case.

"Oh, Kelly, darling, I was the happiest mother in the world when you started going out with Neil," Verna babbled on. "He's every mother's dream of the ideal son-in-law. You were perfect for each other in every way. Why, you wouldn't have had to work another day in your life. He comes from a fine family. I couldn't believe it when you rejected him, and—"

Kelly cut in to correct, "I didn't reject him, Mother. Not then. Let me remind you that I told him I needed to think things over because in all the time we'd been seeing each other, I never once contemplated marriage to him or anybody else. But he wanted to back me into a corner, just like you did, and I wasn't going to be manipulated into a marriage I didn't feel I was ready for. You couldn't accept that, just like you've never been able to accept my making any decisions of my own. Between him pressuring me and you going all to pieces, I was ready to tear my hair out!"

Edie felt the need to divulge, "She was even thinking of running away again, taking a job in another state just to escape all the pressure. I wanted to give her time to calm down, think things out, so—"

"So you talked her into coming here to this God-forsaken place," Verna crisply finished with a scathing glance, coldly adding, "I'd really appreciate it, Edie, if you'd stay out of this. It's between me and *my* daughter."

With a sigh, Edie turned to Kelly. "Maybe it's best

I do butt out.'' She gave her a hug meant to comfort. ''I'm going fishing with Burt today. I'll see you when I get back this evening. Will you be here?''

''Where else would she be?'' Verna cracked, sneering. ''We've got a lot of talking to do, and I expect we'll also be doing some packing. I've made reservations for us to fly home tomorrow. You're welcome to come along, too, Edie, but you'll have to make your own arrangements. I didn't feel you were my responsibility.''

Edie did not trust herself to speak at that point, and, casting another sympathetic glance at Kelly, went inside to gather her things for the day, then left them alone.

Kelly glanced at her watch. Mike would be wondering where she was, but what could she do? Dear Lord, she'd never dreamed her mother would just show up this way, without warning.

Abruptly, Verna demanded, ''Where were you all night, Kelly?''

''Out with friends,'' Kelly hedged, sipping her coffee, wondering how to get away from her long enough to head off Mike, lest he come looking for her.

Verna's eyebrows shot up. ''All night? My goodness, I had no idea there was such wild nightlife on this *idyllic* little island,'' she said with a condescending smirk. ''It was nearly nine o'clock last night by the time I found my way over here, and both you and your grandmother were gone. I sat here and waited awhile but finally had to give up and go back to the hotel. Then, when I got here bright and early this morning, I suspect Edie had just come in herself. What on earth would a woman her age be doing out all night?''

''Maybe you should ask her.''

''I did. And she was just as evasive as you are. Oh, Kelly,'' she implored, ''we can work everything out. I know we can. Don't you want us to be a real family?''

Kelly assured she did but pointed out, ''I've still got

some thinking to do, and I'm not ready to go back just yet.''

Verna gave a nervous laugh. ''What's to think about? You and I had a little tiff because I got upset over having my dream put on hold and my party ruined. I admit now that was silly of me. I overreacted. Even your father said so. All I had to do was explain to everyone how you were called out on an emergency the night before, and Neil hadn't even had a chance to propose yet. It could've all been handled discreetly, easily, and, yes, I could have put that *damned* cake in the freezer,'' she finished with a simpering smile meant to sweep away all tension. ''Neil even said he understands why you reacted like you did and admits he pushed too hard.

''And he does miss you terribly, dear,'' she rushed to emphasize. ''Dodie and Greg have been really concerned. Dodie says he's drinking too much, and she says Larry and Chad told her they're worried, too. He's just afraid he's losing you, and when he told me about the flowers he sent, how you two had such a terrible argument, I knew this had gone on long enough. Then Edie called me the other day and got so huffy, and—''

''Mother, you really had no right to send that embellished message about Dad's being sick. Edie was justified in confronting you after she called the doctor and found out there was nothing to it. I can understand her getting so upset. It was a cruel thing for you to do. You exaggerated, and you know it.'' *Lied*, was more like it, Kelly thought, reluctant to come right out and say so.

Ignoring her censure, Verna went on to say, ''Well, I knew it was time to put an end to this madness, and when Neil heard I was planning to come after you, he wanted to come along, but Dodie and I felt it'd be best he didn't. After all, this is a family matter right now, but I have been thinking since I got here how nice it would be to celebrate our new closeness with a reunion. We can get rooms in Nassau at one of the luxury hotels, and then Neil can come over, and your father. Heaven knows, he needs a vacation, and he's so anxious to see you. And even Dodie and Greg, if they can get away. We can have a big family party.

"Who knows?" she gaily continued, "you and Neil might even get engaged here! Wouldn't that be a nice, romantic story to tell your children, how their parents got engaged in Nassau, and—"

"Stop it, please!" Kelly pressed her hands to her ears, shook her head from side to side, afraid if she didn't ease up, she was going to start screaming and not be able to stop!

Verna's eyebrows shot up. She set aside her coffee mug, stiffly got to her feet. Her mouth set in a thin line, she said, "Very well. We'll go on back tomorrow like I'd planned, and—" she suddenly fell silent, eyes narrowing as she looked beyond Kelly to see the deeply-tanned young man hurrying up the stairs, two steps at a time. He was wearing ragged cut-off jeans, a T-shirt that had seen better days, and sneakers that were hardly holding together. Curiously, she demanded, "*Who* is *that?*"

Kelly braced herself, knew without turning around it would be Mike.

He bounded onto the porch, glanced uncertainly from her to Verna, then said, "We're ready to cast off, and I was wondering what was keeping you."

"My *mother* is keeping me," Kelly said tonelessly, making the introductions. "Mike, my mother. Mother, this is Mike Kramer, my *dive instructor*," she suddenly added.

Mike looked at her sharply. *Dive instructor?* Was that the way she was going to introduce him to her mother? Not that he expected her to confide they were lovers, for crying outloud, but even the term "*friend*" was more personal than "*dive instructor*."

Kelly wanted to bite her tongue the minute she said it, knew by the way Mike was staring at her that he was hurt. But what else could she say?

"Oh, you're learning to dive," Verna cooed. "That's nice. All your friends back home are taking lessons at the Y, you know." She meant Neil, and Kelly knew she meant Neil because they locked eyes and Kelly was warning her not to say more. Verna got the message, just as she didn't need explanation as to what Mike Kramer's *real* status was in Kelly's life. She turned to him then and demurely asked, "Is she a good student?"

He knew, from the little Kelly had confided about her mother, that she wasn't exactly the epitomy of charm and warmth, and he decided it would be best to play along with the way Kelly wanted to handle the unexpected situation. "Yes, she is, and I have to say she's a born diver. I'm very proud of her. She's only one dive away from earning her certification."

"So that's the reason you wanted to stay down here?" Verna pretended to be surprised. "Well, I'm sure you can make that final dive back home." She gave Mike a sweeping look of veiled resentment only he could detect, as she crisply informed, "I've come to take Kelly home. I don't know whether she told you or not, but we've had a few misunderstandings. Her grandmother, I'm afraid, isn't a very good influence on her, and she's caused some problems, but now everything is going to be straightened out."

"Is that so?" Mike went to stand next to Kelly as she leaned against the railing staring moodily out at the turquoise sea beyond, her expression one of suppressed rage. "You're going back with her?"

Verna rushed on, "Yes, and we need to get her

things together, so she won't be diving with you today.''

Kelly drew in her breath, let it out slowly. There were only two things she was sure of in that moment— that she was not leaving with her mother and that she wanted to avoid an angry confrontation over that fact in front of Mike. Turning, she implored him with her eyes to understand. ''Mike, you go ahead with today's dive. My mother and I have a lot of things to talk about. I'll see you when you get back, all right?''

Hesitantly, he nodded. ''Well, sure.'' He started to go but felt the need to confirm they had a date. ''How about dinner?''

Verna was quick to object. ''I thought we'd go on to Nassau this evening. I'm sure we can get a room for just one night.''

Kelly tore wretched eyes from Mike to stare at her and brusquely inform, ''No, *I'm* not leaving today. Or tomorrow, for that matter.''

Verna was stunned, could not, for the moment, respond, told herself it was best to just keep silent, not make a scene in front of a stranger.

Kelly turned back to Mike to assure, ''I'd love to have dinner with you.''

Verna saw her chance, pasted on a dazzling smile and enthusiastically amended, ''Yes, we'd *both* like that. I think it'd be nice for us to get to know each other, Mike. See you tonight.'' She went inside, not sure how long she could maintain her facade of conviviality.

Mike frowned. ''Are you going to be okay?''

''Sure.'' Kelly tried to smile but couldn't. ''See you tonight.'' Doggedly, she got up to also go inside, dreading the evening ahead.

He stared after her a moment before hurrying on his way. Maybe *she* thought it was going to be okay, but he wasn't so sure from his point of view. He hoped he was just worrying needlessly. After all, her mother's arrival had been a shock to her, and by dinner, Kelly would, no doubt, have everything under control. He sure as hell hoped so. It was a volatile situation, and he didn't want to find himself smack dab in the middle.

"Was he the one you were out with all night?" Verna wanted to know as the day wore on.

Kelly had always felt it cowardly to lie. "We went to a party," she hedged. "I've made lots of friends in the short time we've been here."

"*Short time?*" Verna echoed as she fanned herself with a folded newspaper. She found the islands terribly hot and uncomfortably humid. "You've been here nearly a month!"

Had it been that long, Kelly reflected. It certainly didn't seem so, but then she felt somewhat hedonistic because the days and nights blended together in some of the happiest hours she'd ever known.

Verna continued her grilling, seeking to fill in all the blank spaces and suspicions of her mind. "This *Mike*," she said his name as though he were some sort of specimen in question. "Have you known him since you got here?"

Again, Kelly evaded. "I started taking diving lessons right away. It was just something I've always wanted to do."

"You could've gone with Neil and your friends to the Y."

"It's not the same as an open dive, when you actually experience the different colors and shades in the water the deeper you go." Elaborating, caught up in pleasured memories, she went on, more to herself than to her mother, detailing the shipwreck, how it was such a popular attraction for divers.

Verna pressed on. "So, this *Mike* person, you met him and he wanted to give you lessons, and that's what you've been doing every day."

Kelly nodded.

"And now you're having an affair with him."

Kelly sat up straight. She'd been slumped in a chair, watching the lazy roll of the sea, thinking of Mike on the dive, wishing she were with him, but at her mother's unexpected conclusion, she couldn't help but laugh at her choice of words. "An *affair*, did you say? Mother, you make it sound so *wicked!*"

Verna sniffed with disdain. "If you're sleeping with him, then it *is* wicked, and you should be ashamed of yourself. I hope Neil never finds out."

Kelly clenched her teeth.

"Is that all he does? Give diving lessons?"

"He owns his own dive shop, his own house."

"House!" Verna sneered. "From what I've seen, there's nothing around here to brag about owning. Granted, there are lovely homes in Nassau—magnificent homes. Lots of money there. But I think your dive teacher is nothing more than a beach bum, scraping by to make just enough money to afford suntan oil, beer, and hamburgers."

"Maybe . . ." Kelly said tightly, "that's all it takes to make him happy."

"I seem to recall we had this same kind of conversation about another mistake in your life—a mistake named *Len*. He had simple needs, too, only *his* tastes ran to health foods, wine, and a little *marijuana* now and then."

"Clove cigarettes, Mother," Kelly corrected with a sigh. "He was into *clove cigarettes*, not *marijuana*."

"Oh, whatever! But I do think you should've learned your lesson about becoming involved with men who have no money!"

Exasperated, Kelly asked, "How long are we going to spar with each other like this?"

"Till I find out what's going on between you and that . . . that *beach bum!*"

Kelly couldn't take it anymore. She'd had it. "Mike is no beach bum, and this conversation is a waste of time, just like your trip down here, because I'm not going back with you."

"Oh, Kelly, why do you always hurt me this way?" Verna wailed, burrowing her face in her hands and starting to cry. When Kelly did not rush to comfort, she cried louder, harder, and when, at last, she peered between her fingers to gauge her reaction, was infuriated to see she was already down the steps and walking at a fast pace towards the beach.

Furiously wiping at her eyes with the back of her hand, Verna stared after her in silent rage. She wasn't fooling her. That *bohemian* had her snowed. He was the reason she couldn't see how she was throwing her life away by not marrying a wonderful, and *rich*, man like Neil, and Verna fiercely vowed she could not, would not, allow that to happen. By God, she'd find a way to stop it!

When Edie returned late that afternoon, she managed to get Kelly off to herself and let her know she was on her own. "I know you think I'm letting you down, but that's not true. I'm here for you if you need me, but this is something only you can handle. This time, instead of running away, you've got to face up to her, assert yourself, and be ready to pay the price for your actions."

Kelly knew she was right. "I just wish there was some way out of her having dinner with me and Mike tonight. I'm tempted to send word to him I can't go."

Edie admonished, "That's running, Kelly. It doesn't solve anything."

Again, Kelly had to concur and could only hope that through a miracle, the evening might be pleasant, that her mother would ultimately like Mike and approve of him. Yet, she was painfully aware that the chances of that happening were *slim* to *none*.

THIRTEEN

Just before Mike arrived, Verna took a deep breath of resignation and began, "I want you to know that I've been doing a lot of thinking since I got here. I have to admit I was very upset to realize my worst fear was confirmed and you were involved with someone else, but I've decided I have to accept that, and—"

"What's that?" Kelly interrupted, stunned. Her mother had never accepted *anything* about her life that she could remember. She *never* gave up!

Very patiently and distinctly, Verna repeated, "I've decided to accept your relationship with Mike, if that's what makes you happy. After all, as you've pointed out so many times, it *is* your life, to live as you choose. Granted, I think some of the decisions you've made in the past weren't the right ones, but I have to accept that, just as I have to accept this if our family is ever to *be* a family."

Kelly was staring at her, mouth slightly open. Every instinct told her it was a trick, that any minute her mother was going to start wheezing and gasping. "Let me get this straight," she said finally, heart pounding,

"I want to make sure I'm actually hearing that you approve of my relationship with Mike—"

"I didn't say I approved, Kelly," Verna amended, holding up a finger to emphasize the point. "I said I *accept* it, which means I'm not angry, and I'll persuade your father not to be. We'll both accept whatever you decide about your future, with the hope that we can still work on being close."

Kelly pressed on, eyes narrowed with skepticism. "But I told you, I'm planning to move down here for awhile, take a job with Dr. Brewster's clinic in Nassau. If everything works out, I would be moving here permanently, Mother. Can you accept *that?*"

Verna stiffly nodded. She was holding a tissue in her hands and began to nervously pick and shred it. "I would hope," she offered, "that if you do marry this man, that the two of you wouldn't live so far away, that you'd consider coming home."

Kelly knew that could never be the case but with her mother appearing to yield, she didn't want to rock the boat and admit it. Instead, she gingerly offered, "It's too soon to talk about that. Right now, I'm just interested in seeing whether I like it well enough here to stay."

"Well, I just wanted you to know I'll do my best to accept anything you want to do, Kelly. All I want is for us to be close, like a mother and daughter should be. I want to make up for all the lost years."

Kelly accepted her hug awkwardly, sadly thinking how she couldn't recall a time in her life when they'd ever shared a spontaneous embrace.

When Mike arrived, they had a precious moment alone, and after she welcomed his ardent kiss, he searched her face anxiously and asked, "Well, how's it going with your mom?"

"Strangely enough, fine, now that we've had a

chance to talk, but I'm still keeping my fingers crossed she means everything she says about wanting to make peace.''

Mike figured he'd need to cross *toes*, as well. He didn't trust Verna Sanders. If Kelly had never confided a thing about the woman, he still wouldn't turn his back on her. She emanated coldness. She was a snob. And he didn't like her eyes—calculating, mean. But she was Kelly's mother, and he intended to keep his opinion to himself.

Verna greeted him pleasantly by saying, ''Now that my daughter has told me so many wonderful things about you, I'm very anxious for the opportunity to get to know you better.''

''Same here, Mrs. Sanders.'' He mustered his most charming smile, all the while thinking how limp and cool her handshake was.

Anna was thrilled to meet Kelly's mother, and at once began to fuss over them. She even brought a complimentary bottle of Moet, proceeding to tell how grateful she and her family were to Kelly for the way she'd gone out of her way for Winny's dog. ''So now we have a dog named Kelly, who's going to have puppies by a dog named *Biscuit!*'' Laughing and with a mock accusing glance at Mike, she finished, ''And this is Biscuit's owner! He not only gets the pick of the litter, he's going to get the *whole* litter.''

''Hey, that's not fair,'' he laughed. ''Kelly gets to be godmother, so she should have the puppies.''

''One puppy, maybe, if I have a place to keep it,'' she joined in the banter.

Verna struggled to keep a complaisant expression, though she found the conversation ridiculous.

When Winny heard Kelly was there, nothing would do but that she take her by the hand and persuade her to go and check on her namesake. ''I want you to tell me how many puppies she's going to have. So far, I've promised eleven out to my friends.''

Everyone laughed at that, except Verna, who did manage the hint of an indulgent smile. Kelly called to Mike as she was led away, ''See? Winny's taking care of everything. You don't have to worry about raising Biscuit's family, after all.''

Mike watched her disappear into the kitchen, hoped she wouldn't be gone very long. He wasn't exactly comfortable being alone with her mother.

Verna, on the other hand, realized it might be her one and only chance and quickly took advantage of the opportunity to make her play. As soon as Anna left them, she looked him straight in the eye and coolly asked, ''Okay, how much will it take to get you out of my daughter's life?''

He couldn't have been more astonished if she'd slapped his face, and all he could do was sit there and stare at her in disbelief and shock. Then, as she continued to look at him so smugly, arrogantly, he painfully said, ''I think I'll pretend I didn't hear that.''

She lifted the champagne to her lips, took a sip, then riveted her eyes to his. ''Don't play games with me, Mike. I know your type. You pretend to be a refugee from the so-called rat race, and you expound on freedom to do your own thing, free love, peace—an echo from the sixties. But I know you for what you are—a *gigolo*. You probably make very good money at it, too. The diving instructor bit is just a front. So . . .'' she paused for effect, took another swallow of wine, and frostily repeated, ''How much?''

''You're really serious, aren't you?'' He shook his head, incredulous.

''Quite serious. I've been through these escapades with my daughter before. She's very headstrong and rebellious. Unfortunately, her grandmother has a great influence over her, which causes many problems for her father and me. But this time, I'm prepared to do whatever it takes to keep her from messing up her life again. You aren't good enough for her. She deserves better. Now I'm going to be honest and admit I don't have a great deal of money. Probably not what you're used to getting for this sort of thing. But I am prepared to offer you a reasonable amount. Shall we say—five thousand dollars?''

Mike was dumbstruck.

"Oh, very well, then,'' Verna lost some of her bravado. "Seven thousand. That's as high as I can go. Surely, that's adequate, though I'm sure you probably make much more on wealthy older women. Young girls seldom have big bank accounts.'' She reached for her purse. "I didn't bring a lot of cash with me. I had no idea Kelly was in such a mess, but I can write you a check, or, if you don't trust me, I can go to the bank in Nassau first thing tomorrow and get the money.''

Mike shook his head slowly from side to side, eyes growing wide. "You're really serious, aren't you?''

"Oh, stop playing games with me. We both know what you are. Now I'm trying to handle this the easiest way for everyone concerned, but if I have to, I warn you I can get nasty.''

He couldn't resist a smirk and the barb, "How could I tell?''

Her eyes narrowed, mouth tightening into a thin, angry line. "This is your last chance. I promise you that you will never marry my daughter, so you'd best take the money and run while I'm still prepared to finish this quickly and cleanly.''

"If I weren't a gentleman, Mrs. Sanders, I'd tell you exactly where you could stick your money!''

She pursed her lips thoughtfully, bit back her rage over his crude allusion, finally said, "Very well. You leave me no choice. Kelly asked me not to say anything about it, but I think you should know she has a fiance back home, who's not going to be very happy when he hears about this little fling she's been having. Oh, she'll deny it if you ask her about it, swearing it's a ploy on my part to break you up, but I can assure you it's true. We'll even go now to a telephone if you like, and we can call him, and you can talk to him, and he'll tell you himself how they plan to be married when she gets over this latest little escapade. He's quite tolerant because he loves her. I should also point out he comes from a very rich family, and Kelly doesn't want to let him get away until she's sure she could be happy here, with you, living a bohemian lifestyle.

"So you see," she concluded, "my daughter also plays games, and maybe you can now understand my saying I'd like to make this smooth and easy for all of us. We'll just say I'm paying you for the diving lessons you've given my daughter, and I'll take her home to her fiance and never breathe a word about any of this, for her sake."

A great roaring had begun inside, as Mike tried to grasp everything at once. First, he'd been offered a bribe, and that was insult enough—but to be told Kelly was engaged when she'd told him there wasn't anybody else in her life? Damnit, had she lied or was it just another of her mother's tricks to get her way?

Verna was starting to get uneasy. She hadn't figured it would be so difficult. Yet, he sat there, looking like he was ready to lunge across the table to choke the life out of her, and Kelly was going to return any second and want to know what was going on, and what could she say? "Make up your mind, damn you," she hissed then, lip curled back in contempt. "And remember, one word to Kelly, and I'll deny we ever had this conversation, and she'd never believe you, anyway. Blood is thicker than water, you know, and—''

Mike leaped to his feet, the chair falling backwards to hit the floor in a clatter. He didn't know what to think or believe, knew only that he had to get out of there fast, before he said or did something he'd surely regret.

Kelly walked out of the kitchen in time to see him storming out the front door. She started after him, to see what was going on, then heard the familiar sound of gasping and wheezing, turned to see her mother struggling to breathe amidst wild sobbing. Other diners were hurrying to her aid.

"Let me through," Kelly yelled, rushed to kneel beside her chair and urged, "Mother, calm down. Get hold of yourself."

Someone yelled to get a doctor, but Verna raised a feeble hand in protest, "No. I just need my pills . . . left them at the hotel. Take me there, please . . .''

Kelly wasn't taking a chance the attack was faked. She wanted to go after Mike to find out why he'd charged out in an angry rush but didn't dare take the time just then.

A man from a nearby table offered to drive them to the Sea Gull in his car, and Kelly gratefully accepted. On the way, Verna alternately wheezed and cried, attempting to relate the terrible scene with Mike. "Never . . . never has anyone . . . said such ugly things to me . . .''

Kelly told her not to talk, to wait till they got her pills, got her into bed.

When, at last, she was settled, Verna had managed to conjure a tale of how she'd only asked Mike a few questions about himself, and he had become indignant and verbally abusive.

Kelly didn't want to risk upsetting her again, yet it

was difficult to believe that of Mike. Humoring her, she offered, "I'll go find him and talk to him, Mother, and I'll ask him why he reacted like that. You just try to get some sleep."

Verna threw her arms around her, began to sob wildly, begging, "No, please don't leave me here alone. I'm in a strange place, without my doctor, and I'm frightened. Stay with me, please, Kelly."

Kelly sighed, knew she was trapped. "All right," she said finally, "but I don't want you talking anymore, okay? You go to sleep, and I'll stay with you."

Verna sniffed, lay back on the pillows, reached to pat her cheek lovingly as she whispered, "I want you to know I love you, Kelly. You're my baby. My only baby. I nearly died having you, and I'd have gladly done so to give you life. You're everything to me, and all I want before I do have to leave this earth is for us to be close, at last. Go home with me, please. I love you too much to tell you what that terrible man said, but I will tell you that you're living in a fool's paradise if you think you can ever be happy with someone like that."

"Mother, if you don't stop talking and go to sleep," Kelly sharply interrupted, "I'm going to leave you. I mean it. Now isn't the time to talk about any of this."

"Very well," Verna sniffed, closing her eyes in resignation. She was fairly confident she'd won, anyway.

Finally, with her mother asleep, at last, Kelly went to sit in the chair by the window and stare out at the night, wondering what did happen when she left the two of them alone. None of it sounded like Mike. Desperately, she wanted to find him but knew, sadly, she was trapped till morning.

It was nearly midnight, and Kelly had dozed off in the chair when she awakened at once to the sound of soft tapping at the door. Rushing to open it, hoping against hope it would be Mike, she was still relieved to find Edie standing there.

Glancing inside the room and seeing that Verna appeared to be sleeping, Edie drew Kelly out into the hallway to whisper, "Burt and I stopped by the Mariner for a nightcap, and Anna told me what little she knew—that Mike charged out mad as a hornet and Verna had an attack. What's the real story?"

"That's all I know," Kelly hated to helplessly admit. "She claims Mike said something terrible to her that upset her so bad she went all to pieces. I haven't been able to get away to go find him and hear his side. Mother made me promise to stay here with her tonight, says she's scared to be alone."

"I can stay with her. You go find Mike."

"Would you mind?" Kelly felt a rush of hope. "She really won't like it if she wakes up and finds you here, but I really need to talk to him."

"Of course, you do. Now I left Burt waiting downstairs in his pickup truck. You go tell him I said for him to take you to find him. You can't be running around the island this time of night on a motor scooter."

Kelly hugged her, tears of gratitude sparkling in her eyes. "Edie, you're the greatest." Then, seeing the almost sad way she was looking at her, anxiously asked, "What's wrong?"

Reluctantly, Edie attempted to tell her. "It's just that you're on your own now, Kelly. I can't, and won't, do anything else for you in this instance."

Kelly shook her head, not understanding. "What are you talking about?"

"I've given you all the advice I intend to. I've tried to point out to you how your impetuousness, your rebellion, has led you to make some mistakes in your life. It's time now for you to think for yourself, make your own decisions, and be prepared to pay the price, whether right or wrong. You're a grown woman, and it's your life. Live it with the courage of your own convictions.''

With that, she stepped into Verna's room, quietly closed the door in Kelly's face, leaving her in the hallway to ponder all she'd said.

Burt Grady politely asked no questions when Kelly told him she needed to find Mike, merely said he'd noticed the lights earlier on the *Free Spirit*, which was tied up at the dock. He took her there.

She found him sitting out on the deck, staring at the dark abyss that was the sea and horizon blended. He was nursing a beer, didn't look up as she came onboard.

''Mike, we need to talk,'' she began softly, wishing she could just run and throw herself into his arms.

He did not immediately respond, and when he did, it was curt. ''Yeah. I guess we do.''

He was sitting on a folding chair, and she waved away his offer to relinquish it as she dropped to sit on the deck nearby. ''No, this is fine.'' She took a deep breath, began, ''All I know about this crazy mess is Mother had one of her attacks because something happened between you two while I wasn't there. She said you got angry with her.''

He glanced at her sharply in the dim light, challenged, ''Oh, really? And just what did she say I got angry *about?*''

''She didn't. That's what I'm here to find out. Mike, I know only too well how antagonistic and hard to get along with she can be. Whatever it was, I have to know, so I can get this straightened out. I mean . . .'' she gestured helplessly, baffled by it all. ''Earlier, I dared to think she might really be sincere in wanting us to be close, that she was, at long last, going to stop trying to run my life. Whatever happened to make things blow up? Tell me, please . . ." she implored.

Mike turned his gaze once more into the darkness beyond.

She pushed. "Mike, *talk* to me."

He crushed the can in a clink of tin and a splatter of stale beer. She jumped but made no sound. Finally, resolutely, he told her, "I'm staying out of your family problems, Kelly."

She blinked, more confused than ever. "But I have to know what happened back there that set her off. What did you say to her? What did *she* say to *you?*" Moving closer to him, she placed her hands on his knees as she stared up at his stormy face. "Mike, if you love me, help me with this."

Adamantly, he shook his head. "How I feel about you hasn't got anything to do with not wanting to be in the middle." Teeth clamped together so tightly his jaws ached, he reminded himself of the vow he'd spent the last few hours repeating over and over. No way was he going to hurt her by letting her know her mother had tried to buy him off like a goddamn gigolo!

"First Edie tells me she's butting out of my life, now you," Kelly snapped then. "What am I supposed to do? Read people's minds? I'd like to get this straightened out, Mike, because I do love you, and I'd like to believe we *can* build a future together, but I also want to make peace with my mother if there's any way possible. She came all the way down here because, in her way, she loves me. But I can't do anything till I find out what upset her so."

"Why don't you ask her?"

"She doesn't want to tell me. She says it's too awful."

With a bitter laugh, he asked, "And you believe that?"

Pounding his knees with her fists in frustration, she cried, "Damnit, Mike, I don't know what to believe anymore."

"I didn't start the war, so I'm not getting involved in the combat. But tell me . . ." he reached to cup her chin in his hand, forcing her to meet his fiery gaze. "Were you telling me the truth when you said you weren't involved with anybody else?"

That was a jolt, and suddenly, she knew. Her mother must've said something about Neil, and Mike got mad. Feeling no guilt, she soberly replied, "I told you before. I'm a free agent."

He looked at her thoughtfully, trying to decipher whether he saw truth, or lies, in her face, instead perceived only indignity and anger. "Maybe," he said with a sigh of finality, getting slowly to his feet as she scrambled to stand beside him, "we'd better call it a night. We can talk about this tomorrow when we both aren't so keyed up and tired."

She was bitterly disappointed he apparently didn't care enough to try to settle things between them then and there. "Sure, fine, if that's the way you want it." Stiffly, with chin lifted in a gesture of composure she did not truly feel at that moment, she blinked back frustrated tears and hurried across the deck to step out and onto the pier.

He watched her thoughtfully, knew she was upset. "Kelly, wait a minute," he called after her. "Don't go off mad. You've got to understand that I just don't want to be in the middle of the situation between you and your mother."

She kept on walking.

He shook his head, didn't know what else he could do. He'd be damned if he'd tell her what had happened. Attempting once more to soothe, he called, "At least let me drive you to the cottage."

"Thanks, but no thanks." She headed across the sand in the direction of the hotel, not bothering to tell him where she was going. Perhaps, she thought with a wave of humiliation, her mother was right, and she was, in fact, living in a *fool's paradise!*

Mike, disconsolately stared after her. He'd had some questions of his own he wanted answered but didn't feel either of them was in the mood to discuss them right then.

Maybe, he thought miserably, it had all been a mistake from the beginning, anyway.

And maybe he was a fool to think they could have had a future together.

Yet, despite all doubts and fears and revelations, he couldn't deny he did love her deeply.

FOURTEEN

When Kelly reached the hotel, she mournfully told Edie she hadn't been able to get Mike to tell her anything. "I don't know anymore than I did, but one thing is for sure—something sure set her off, and now Mike and I are snapping at each other."

"Try not to worry. It's late. Everybody is tired." Edie nodded to Verna, who was sleeping soundly. "I've got a sneaky suspicion those pills she takes are heavy tranquilizers. Walter is no fool. He's probably figured out himself by now she's faking those attacks and got her doctor to prescribe something to shut her up for awhile. I'll see you tomorrow."

"And how are you going to get back to the cottage? It's late—"

"Not to worry," she assured, gave her a quick hug in parting. "Burt came back after he left you at the pier and said he was leaving his truck for me."

"You know how to drive a pickup truck?" Kelly was dubious.

Edie laughed softly. "Honey, I promised myself when your grandfather died that I was going to spend the rest of my life trying out everything I'd missed in life. Driving a pickup truck is one of them! See you later.''

For a long time, Kelly just sat at the window, gazing out into the night, trying to figure out what to do. Maybe Edie was trying to make her see it was time she faced life, rather than run from it, and she could also understand Mike's reluctance to say anything unkind about her mother. Still, she would've liked a little support.

Finally, exhausted, she slept, awaking only when she heard the door opening and closing. She sat straight up, feeling stiff from having curled up in the chair, shook her head to clear it as she groggily struggled to remember where she was and why. It all came flooding back as she saw her mother standing beside the bed.

Dressed in a summer suit and low heels, Verna was busily packing her suitcase.

"What are you doing? Do you feel okay?"

"I feel much better this morning, and I didn't mean to wake you. You seemed to be sleeping so well.''

Kelly was puzzled by the way she was smiling at her, so . . . so *fondly*, as though the night before hadn't happened at all, and everything was going to be okay. Then, the fact she *was* packing soaked in. "Are you going somewhere?"

"Yes," she brightly confirmed. "I was on the phone bright and early this morning confirming my reservation.''

"But, I thought—"

"You thought I was going to stay on," she finished for her, then continued, "Well, frankly, so did I, or, at least long enough to talk you into going back with me, but after last night, I think it's best if I just get on back to my world and leave you to yours.'' She looked at her in pity, shook her head. "I've done all I can do. Maybe I've done too much all these years, but you can't blame a mother for trying. At least I'll deserve a star in my crown for my efforts.''

Kelly was relieved and not about to beg her to change her mind. Still, she wanted some answers. ''Mother, I'd like to know exactly what Mike said to you last night that upset you so.''

''Ask him.''

''I did.''

Verna glanced about sharply, wanted to know, ''When did you talk to him?''

She saw no reason not to tell her that Edie came by and stayed with her so she could go talk to him. ''But he won't tell me,'' she hated to admit. ''He says he doesn't want to be in the middle.''

Verna thought that odd but was relieved. She'd been prepared to deny the whole conversation. ''Well, he's right. He shouldn't. And it's best we just forget it.''

Hoping to catch her off-guard, Kelly watched her face intensely as she quickly asked, ''What did you tell him about Neil?''

Verna was expressionless. After all, she'd been expecting this confrontation and psyched herself up to be very in control. She countered, ''Did he say I said anything about Neil?''

''No, but he asked me if I were involved with anybody back home—*again*. I'd already told him before that I'm not. Since he brought it up, I thought maybe you'd said something.''

She turned to stare at her incredulously. ''Why on earth did you lie to him?''

''I wasn't lying. Any 'strings' are from Neil's point of view, not mine. There was nothing to tell.''

Verna picked up her purse. ''Well, it's your business from now on. I've got to be heading for Nassau and the airport. All I've got to say is that I hope you know what you're doing, dear. I'm just afraid my health won't let me keep trying to save you from yourself.''

She leaned to kiss her cheek, and Kelly fought to keep from turning away. Why couldn't she just go on a pleasant note without leaving a sarcastic echo? Following her downstairs and carrying her bag for her, she asked one last time, ''I wish you'd tell me what happened last night.''

''What difference does it make? If I told you, you'd jump on him about it, and he'd probably deny it, and I figure sooner or later you'll come to your senses, anyway, and realize he's not for you, so why dwell on it?''

Reeta had made arrangements for Verna to have transportation to Nassau, and a car and driver were waiting to take her to the waterfront for passage by boat. She gave Kelly a hug in parting, blinked back tears of regret and whispered, ''Hurry home, dear, to your family who loves you dearly.'' Then she was gone.

Kelly was even more puzzled. It wasn't like her mother to retreat, not without a fight, and certainly not without a big blow-up. And what was she supposed to do now? There was trouble in paradise because she and Mike were surely at odds. But maybe, she tried to pump herself up, it would blow over. Maybe last night hadn't meant anything, and her mother had just had one of her fits. That wouldn't surprise her at all. Mike was doing the gentlemanly thing to stay out of it, probably figured if he did, it'd soon be forgotten. Kelly decided maybe it was best not to dwell on it, pretend it had never happened, and just get on with her life and be glad her mother was out of it for the time being.

She went to the cottage for a shower and change of clothes. Edie was nowhere around, which meant she'd probably gone off for a day of deep-sea fishing with Burt.

Anxious to see if things could be smoothed over after last night, Kelly went on to Mike's dive shop but saw the *Closed* sign on the door, which meant he was gone for the day. She was disappointed at his taking off with a rift still between them. The *Free Spirit* wasn't at the pier, but he had no dive scheduled. She was sure of that; she'd seen his reservation book the day before. Besides, he'd promised she could go on the next dive because it was all she needed to get her certification. Maybe now, though, she reflected sadly, he didn't care about keeping that promise anymore than he cared how upset she'd been the night before.

For awhile, Kelly just walked aimlessly up and down the beach, lost in thought. Was she really a fool to think she and Mike could be happy on a permanent basis? And how could she know, for sure, whether it was really and truly love she was feeling—and not just infatuation because of the wonderworld they were living in? The lovemaking was fabulous, the best she'd ever known. And Mike was handsome and charming, had swept her off her feet as no one else ever had. But was it real? So many questions—and no one to answer them except herself, and she just didn't feel too self-confident at the moment.

Around lunchtime, she went to the cottage, got a can of Coke, and then sat down on the porch to stare out at the eternal sea. She hadn't been there long when Edie showed, and she was overjoyed, saying she was afraid she'd be gone all day.

Edie was relieved to hear Verna had left but also a bit suspicious. "She's up to something. I've never known her to give up, especially when she's mad about something, and from what you say, she was really rabid last night. Have you talked to Mike today?"

"I can't find him."

"Well, I think he's probably as upset as you are. We saw him this morning as we were leaving. He was sitting on his boat, looking like he'd lost his last friend."

"I can't do anything about that. He refuses to tell me what happened, so what am I supposed to do?"

Edie shrugged. "Like I told you, it's time you made your own decisions, but if you want my opinion, I admire Mike for staying out of it. After all, I doubt he's got anything nice to say about her, and it's to his credit not to criticize your mother—*no matter how much she deserves it*," she couldn't resist scornfully adding.

"Well, she's gone, and the thing to do now is try to put it all behind, I guess." She stood. "I think I'll walk down to his shop again, and if he's not there, I'll rent a Moped and ride out to his cottage. Then I'm going over to Nassau and talk to Dr. Brewster and see if he still wants to hire me. By the way, have you decided whether you want to stay on with me?" she asked, starting on down the steps. When Edie didn't respond, she turned, waited.

"Haven't decided just yet," she finally said. "You'll do fine on your own, if I don't."

So that was it, Kelly fumed, continuing on her way. Obviously, Edie had already decided she was going back, and that was why she said she was staying out of things from now on. Why should she care? She wasn't going to be here, anyway. Kelly was really starting to feel all alone.

Mike's boat was still out, and when she went to his cottage, he wasn't there, either.

Deciding to go on into Nassau and talk with Dr. Brewster, she wound up helping at the clinic for the rest of the day. He assured her she had a job any time she wanted one, and when the clinic closed, insisted she go home to meet his family and have dinner. It was nearly midnight when they took her back to Harbour Island in their cabin cruiser.

Exhausted, she went to bed, not at all surprised that Edie was still out. She wasn't around the next morning, either, so Kelly went immediately in search of Mike, burning with the desire to talk to him. Her heart was aching. They had shared something special, and even though she was assailed with doubts after all that had happened, she could not just turn her back and walk away without trying to talk about it.

Mike's boat was still out, and she decided to go to the Mariner for breakfast. It was nearly empty, so Anna brought her coffee over and sat down. "I was really worried about your mother the other night," she began, "but I understand she's gone home."

"Who told you that?" Kelly wanted to know.

"Reeta. She told me when she came by late last night looking for Mike."

Kelly felt like she'd got herself involved in a game of *Twenty Questions*, anxiously urged, "Well, go on. I've been looking for him myself. What did she want with him?"

"Seems some people are coming in from the states especially to dive at the shipwreck. They're flying in to Nassau by charter plane and called long distance to make reservations at the Sea Gull. When they couldn't get in touch with Mike at his number at the dive shop, they called back and told Reeta they were concerned he might be gone when they got here. So, she was out looking for him to confirm he'd take them on the dive."

"And?" she anxiously gestured for her to continue. "Where did she find him?"

Anna tossed down the rest of her coffee, gave a helpless shrug. "She didn't. He's off on his boat. So she talked to Ronnie, and he said not to worry, that Mike had probably gone off to one of his other shops to check on things. He looked in his book and saw he didn't have a dive scheduled till tomorrow, and that was for you and him to go to the shipwreck, anyway, because he told Ronnie he was taking you down for your last open dive so you'd be certified and wanted him to go along. Ronnie told her then to just tell those people to come on in because Mike is sure to be back by then. They can dive with you—''

Kelly interrupted then, had barely paid attention to anything after the part about Mike probably going to one of his *other shops*. ''What are you talking about? What other shops?''

Anna blinked in surprise. ''You mean he never told you? He's got shops on other islands. I've never been to any of them, but Ronnie goes with him once in awhile, and he says they're nice and do quite well. He didn't tell you?'' she repeated incredulously.

Kelly absently shook her head, murmured, ''No, he didn't.'' Then, more to herself than to Anna, ''Seems there's lots of things Mike doesn't want to tell me.''

Abruptly, she got up and walked out, leaving Anna staring after her in wonder.

It was late afternoon when Kelly found Mike at his shop. He was busy checking air tanks. He glanced up as she entered, and there was no mistaking the pleasure in his eyes over seeing her there.

Hoping she was in a better mood and that they could just forget all that had happened, he warmly greeted, ''I hope you don't mind having company on your big dive tomorrow. Some rich tourists are coming in by chartered plane, specifically for the shipwreck. Ronnie went ahead and set it up for them to go with us.''

''I heard,'' she made her voice perky, ''and I'm looking forward to it. I'll finally graduate.'' She was unnerved by his nearness, all the feelings she held for him whirling inside.

He patted the stool beside him, offered a shy grin, and inquired lightly, "Still mad at me?"

"Still *confused*," she countered.

He didn't pick up on that, instead continued to try to ease the tension between them. "So how have you been?"

She wanted him to know, "Mom went home yesterday."

"Yeah, I heard." He couldn't resist adding, "I guess it's a relief she wasn't as sick as she appeared to be the other night."

Kelly didn't comment on that, instead remarked, "Well, I guess I'll never know what happened between you two because she refused to say anything, either."

"Well, some things are better left unsaid. I'm just glad it's over."

Suddenly she couldn't help herself and was compelled to ask, "How *much* is over, Mike? Does that include a part of what we had?"

He laid aside the tank he was working on, turned to face her solemnly, thoughtfully. He ached to reach out and touch her but resisted. Instead, he asked a question of his own, "Do you want it to be?"

"I'm asking you, Mike. I want you to know I'm hurt by the way you acted the other night. I came to you because I wanted help with a terrible situation, and you turned your back on me. Is that how you treat someone you say you love?"

He was thoughtful for a moment. He didn't like the way the conversation was going, but he was torn by it all and didn't know how to react. Her mother had handed him a pretty big insult, and he was still unsure about Kelly's supposed fiance and knew she wasn't going to tell him anymore than she already had, which was to deny. The bottom line, though, was that he knew, without a doubt, that he loved her, but things had gone into a tailspin, and it was just up to her to decide when the spinning would stop. Finally, he offered, "Like I told you then, Kelly, how I feel about you had nothing to do with it. What good would it have done for me to tell you what went on? It would've just made matters worse. Now she's gone, and you're here, and frankly, I'd like for us to try to get things back like they were before she came."

Kelly still had her doubts, sired by her mother's remark about living in a fool's paradise. And the burning question still nagged within as to whether she could truly be a part of Mike's world. "We can try," she said in a small, tight voice, wishing she could sound more positive, *be* more positive, but something she could not understand was holding her back. She was sure she loved him, yet could not give one hundred percent.

Mike sensed her indecision and swallowed against his rising fury. If she loved him, why didn't she go ahead and say to hell with all the negatives? Why was she holding back? What was her problem?

The door opened, and he tore himself away from his misery, couldn't mask the annoyance over being interrupted at such a time. He looked at the man grinning so arrogantly, saw how, as he flicked his gaze over Kelly, that his expression changed to—what? Anger? Indignation? Kelly wasn't looking at him, not then. She was still lost in her own thoughts. "Yes, what is it?" Mike warily got to his feet as he noticed the way the intruder had begun to clench and unclench his fists, like he was just about to explode.

"Hello, Kelly," the stranger said tightly.

She turned then, and Mike saw the way the blood drained from her face. Her lips moved but no sound came, and her eyes grew wide with first surprise, then flashed with anger. "What . . . what are you doing here?" she stammered then, scrambling off the stool.

Mike instinctively stepped between them. "Who is this guy?"

"*Who am I?*" The stranger laughed, but it was not a nice sound. It was cold and harsh, as was his expression. "You mean she hasn't told you about me?"

Kelly raised her hand in protest. "Neil, how dare you—"

Mike interrupted, his own fury exploding. "Is this the so-called *fiance* your mother told me about?"

Kelly whirled on him then. "So she *did* say something to you about it!"

"You better damn well know she did, and I asked you about it, and you said there wasn't anybody else."

At that, Neil cried in disbelief, "Kelly, how could you say such a thing? My God, honey, after what we had together? Do you think I'd have gone out and spent nearly five grand on a diamond ring if we didn't have something going?"

Mike was really starting to boil. He ached to smash his fist in the guy's face, but if Kelly *was* lying, then it wasn't his fault. Still, he feared he'd lose control if he kept running his mouth. "Tell you what, buddy," he pointed a finger at the door, the nerves in his jaw tightening, veins in his neck standing out as anger mounted. "I think it'd be best if you got on out of here and let me and Kelly get a few things straight."

"No," Neil shook his head adamantly. "I just got in, and I haven't seen her in awhile, and we need to talk just now. What's your part in all this, anyway? Oh, I know!" He snapped his fingers dramatically and sneered, "You're the beach bum her mother told me she was having a fling with, and I'm afraid you also happen to be the guy me and my friends have booked a dive with for tomorrow.''

''You!'' Kelly cried. ''You and Mother set this up, didn't you?''

He shrugged. ''No reason you shouldn't know, honey. Verna called me from here and said she thought it was best I come on down and get you. She also told me how you'd been taking dive lessons and how you went on and on about some shipwreck. So Larry knows this guy with his own plane, and he likes to dive, too, so him and Chad and me decided to make a little vacation out of bringing you home.''

Mike couldn't trust himself to keep his temper under control any longer. ''You two work it out then. I'm out of here.''

He pushed by Neil and stormed out of the shop, heading towards his boat. Kelly was right behind him, and when Neil tried to hold her back, she whirled on him in such savage rage he jumped back, lest she physically attack. ''I'll talk to *you* later. Right now, just get out of my face!''

She caught up with Mike as he was working furiously to untie his boat from the pier. ''You've got to listen to me,'' she pleaded. ''It's not like it looks. I never lied to you. Neil jumped to conclusions. I never made any promises, any commitments.''

''Oh, yeah?'' he challenged. ''Seems like you're the only one who sees it that way.''

''You have to know the way he is, and the way my mother is. They're both used to getting their own way, and when she came down here and found out about us, she cooked up this scheme with him over long distance to try to break us up.''

He had untied the rope but held onto the top of the piling with both hands as he leaned forward to irately inform her, ''I think you told me what you thought I wanted to hear. All along, when I was falling in love with you, I never once misled you. Neither did I lead you on. So why couldn't you have been honest with me and told me how there was this guy back in North Carolina who considered himself your fiancé?''

"He is not my fiancé!" she furiously cried in denial.

"Well, whatever he is to you doesn't matter now because . . ." He pushed off from the pier, "I see you never loved me. Frankly, I don't think you've got the guts it takes to love anybody. You aren't willing to pay the price."

"And what's that supposed to mean?"

"You figure it out." He moved to start the engine. "Now go talk to your boyfriend. Tell him if he still wants to dive tomorrow, it's on."

"I'm surprised you still want to go," she yelled.

"Hey!" He turned to hold up his arms in a gesture of helplessness. "I'm the beach bum! Your mother said so! I need all the help I can get. Who am I to turn down four dive fees?"

"Well, I'm going, too, damnit! I've got one more dive coming to me, and I sure paid a high price for *my* lessons!" At that, she turned and walked briskly back up the pier.

Biscuit was standing in the sand, watching with mournful eyes. "Hey, boy," she said through a mist of tears. "You believe me, don't you?"

Biscuit's lips turned back in a menacing snarl, then he raced by her at full speed, running all the way to the end of the pier to make a dramatic leap, landing on his master's boat. Kelly stared after him, muttered, "You're *man's* best friend, all right. So who the hell have *I* got to lean on?"

She didn't have to look far to find Neil. He, Larry, Chad, and a man she didn't know, probably the owner and pilot of their plane, were in the bar just down the beach from the dive shop. She walked in, waited for her eyes to adjust to the semi-darkness, then saw them gathered at the bar. Neil was telling a story, gesturing with his hands. The others were laughing but fell silent when they spotted Kelly heading in their direction.

Neil looked around to see what was going on, then took a deep breath, readied himself for the confrontation.

Icily, she said, "You want it here or outside?"

Astonished, his laugh was more of a gasp, as he looked to his friends for support, quipping, "Hey, are we talking about a barroom brawl, or what? I mean, why don't you just ask me to step out in the alley?"

The others exchanged nervous glances.

"The alley. Here. It doesn't matter to me, but I'm not sure you want your pals to hear what I've got to say to you."

He slid off the stool, grabbed her arm, which she promptly shook off, and snarled, "Oh, hell. Come on. Let's get your tantrum over with."

She led the way to the outdoor bar on the beach side of the building, which was vacant for the moment. Trying to keep her cool, she began, "It won't work, Neil. You should've realized I won't be victimized."

Irritably, he flashed, "What the hell are you talking about? We chartered a plane to come down here and go diving and hoped you'd be ready to quit acting like a brat and come home with us. How do you figure that's *victimizing* you?"

"You thought if you put me on the spot I'd give in, just like you planned that night at the lake, but you can forget it. I'm not leaving."

He snickered. "Well, you might as well go back with us now because from the way your beach bum lover boy acted back there, I'd say there's no reason for you to stay here."

"That," she effusively fired, "hasn't got anything to do with my staying, so I suggest you and your friends leave now."

"Oh, no," he shook his head. "We came to dive. We spent a lot of money on this trip, and we're not leaving till we get good and ready. And you know something else, Kelly?"

She saw the way he was reeling, realized what she'd not seen due to her anger till now—*he was drunk!*

"I'll tell you something . . ." he wagged his finger at her, rocking back and forth on his heels. "I loved you. Really loved you. You were everything a man could want in a wife. Even when your mother told me I had some competition, I figured—*what the hell?* Kelly's got a right to sow her oats before we settle down. I'll just boogie on down there and bring her home. Boy, was I a fool!"

With a pitying sigh, she told him, "I'm afraid I could never live up to your expectations of the perfect wife. I dearly hope you find someone who can. But get something straight, *dude!*" Her rage returned. "It's over! No more cute stuff. You stay and dive tomorrow if you want to, but no funny business. We're finished. Kaput! Got that?"

"Oh, yeah, baby, you don't have to worry about that," he hiccupped, sneered, hiccupped again.

Kelly had enough. She turned and started walking across the pink-tinted sand. When he sobered up, it'd start all over again. She'd never realized it before but Neil was a spoiled brat and couldn't take no for an answer.

In that moment, she was sure of only one thing— she would make that dive. There'd be time later to decide what she was going to do with the rest of her life!

"I don't believe it!" Edie stared at Kelly, wide-eyed. "I just don't believe it! I knew Verna was sneaky, conniving, would stop at nothing to get her own way, but this takes the cake. She actually sneaked out of the hotel before you woke up to call Neil and get him to come down here, thinking if he did, he'd embarrass you into going home with him."

"That was only part of it. I think she was also wanting to show up Mike, wanting me to see the difference between him and Neil as to financial and social background. I was supposed to make a comparison between Mike in his cutoff jeans and tank top, and Neil in his neat shorts and Alexander Julian pullover knit. I was supposed to be impressed by Neil popping in by chartered plane with his *jet-set* friends, and . . . oh!" She threw up her hands in frustration. They were sitting on the porch at the cottage, and she got up to pace about in agitation. "It just makes me so mad! I wish now I'd never come here! I should've just taken that job in Texas and got the hell away from home, once and for all. Everything I try to do in life gets screwed up."

"Well, what do you plan to do now?"

Kelly explained that she wanted to make the dive to finish out the requirements for her certification. "Then I think I'll move over to Nassau and work for Dr. Brewster for awhile. I haven't really decided."

"What about Mike?"

Kelly shrugged with feigned indifference, even though her heart was pounding at just the mention of his name. "What about him?"

"Aren't you in love with him?"

"Maybe. But I'm going on a sabbatical from love for awhile. I worked hard to get my degree, and I think

I'd be wiser to concentrate on my career instead of my personal life. Besides,'' she added cynically, ''love screws everything up and makes life crazy and complicated.''

''I suppose so. It also makes life fun and interesting,'' Edie murmured softly, then asked, ''What about this place? If you're breaking it all off with Mike, it'd probably be better if we vacated.''

''You're right. How about if we get Burt to run us over to Nassau this afternoon to look for a place? We can pack up tonight and leave after my dive tomorrow.''

Edie didn't say anything.

Kelly realized she suddenly seemed nervous. No doubt, she was homesick and ready to go back to her townhouse and her life in Charlotte and didn't want to admit it for fear she'd be letting her down at a time when her world seemed to be crumbling, anyway. Kelly decided to make it easy on her. ''Look, you shouldn't feel obligated to stay down here with me. I may be coming home in a few weeks, anyway. I just need some time alone before facing Mom again. I'm so mad and disgusted with her right now, we'd just have a big fight and she'd go into one of her attacks and wind up in the hospital again. I can get a place by myself, work for Dr. Brewster while I make up my mind where I'd like to go from here. You go on back and don't worry about me.''

Edie had a dreamy, faraway look on her face as she quietly declared, ''Oh, I'm not going back, Kelly. I've decided I'm going to make *my* life crazy and complicated.''

Kelly could only stare at her, absolutely baffled. Was she getting senile, as her mother accused? She surely wasn't making sense right then.

Edie raised shining eyes to meet Kelly's curious stare

before continuing, "And I'm also going to make my life *fun* and *interesting*."

Kelly gave an exasperated sigh. "What *are* you talking about?"

"The brass ring I told you about, the one you have to just reach out and grab if you want to get the most out of living. I'm going to go for it!" She giggled mysteriously, then confided in a voice trembling with excitement, "Burt asked me to marry him, Kelly, and I said yes!"

FIFTEEN

Mike was tempted to call off the dive but knew he'd look like a jealous fool if he did. Ordinarily, he didn't give a damn what people thought, but this was different. Neil Brandon would run his mouth to anybody on the island who would listen before he left, recounting how he and his buddies had flown all the way to the Bahamas from North Carolina, thinking they had a dive trip all set, only to find out they'd wasted time and money because Mike Kramer was being a jerk. He told himself, too, that he needed to honor the commitment for Kelly's sake. She'd worked hard, deserved to be certified. Yet he couldn't deny the bottom line was that he loved her more than he'd thought it was possible to love any woman. He'd lain awake most of the night mulling over everything that had happened. He just couldn't see where he might have done anything different. He'd let her know he cared about her, that he wanted her to stay. Sure, he'd been tempted to come right out and ask her to marry him but wanted her to love the island life for her own reasons, not just because of him. That way, she'd never blame him if she got

homesick, and it wouldn't eat away at their relationship. He tried, too, during the long, miserable hours,
to understand why she hadn't told him the truth about
Neil Brandon. Could it be that she was being honest?
That it had all been one-sided? He was willing to give
her the benefit of the doubt on that one, but it looked
like they were history, anyway. He couldn't do anything now. Kelly still held the cards. How she played
the hand was up to her.

The morning dawned with blue skies, no clouds, a
brilliant sun, and the water crystal clear and calm. A
perfect day for scuba diving. Ronnie arrived promptly
at nine o'clock, and Mike left him to make sure everything was ready on the *Free Spirit*, then went to the
shop.

He saw that Neil and his buddies were already waiting outside. Neil had a smirky look on his face. The
others looked pleasant enough, obviously excited over
the outing. They were wearing swim trunks, carrying
their own face masks and fins. Unlocking the door, he
motioned them inside. Brusquely, he informed, "I'll
need to look at your '*C*' cards."

Neil snickered. "Do you really think we'd be dumb
enough to come this far and book this dive if we aren't
certified?"

The others exchanged uncomfortable glances. After
the angry encounter with Kelly the night before, they'd
spent the rest of the evening getting him calmed down.
He'd promised to behave on the dive, not make any
trouble.

Mike didn't look at him, just snapped, "Show me
your card, Brandon, or you don't dive."

Attempting to keep the two from a confrontation,
Chad spoke up to ask, "How deep is the shipwreck,
Kramer?"

Mike was looking over the cards. "Eighty feet.

Don't worry. You're within the sport diving limit of a hundred, and I see by these cards that's the class you're all certified for.''

Ignoring the disapproving glares of his friends, Neil coldly asked, ''What about you? What are *your* qualifications? If I'm going down eighty feet in the ocean, I want to make sure the guy leading the way knows what he's doing.''

The others softly groaned among themselves, while Mike made direct eye contact with Neil as he icily informed, ''The *guy* leading the way is certified by the Professional Association of Diving Instructors as a Dive Master *and* a Master Scuba Diver. Does that make you feel secure enough?''

Chad spoke up again, ''Sure does, Kramer.'' Giving Neil a jab with his elbow, he urged, ''Hey, cool it. The rest of us came here to dive. If you got a problem, why don't you just wait at the hotel?''

Mike seized the opportunity to say, ''It can be dangerous down there, Brandon. If you can't leave your personal feelings topside, then I'm not taking you down.''

Neil clamped his teeth together, slowly counted to ten, then forced a grin, glancing around at everyone as he shrugged, said, ''Hey, I have a right to make sure he knows what he's doing okay? Now that I do, everything's fine. No problems.''

Mike hoped he meant it. He wanted to know, ''Where'd you guys make your open dives? According to your 'C,' you've only been certified a month. You can't have much experience beyond your required dives.''

Jay Morton, owner of the plane and pilot, spoke for the first time. ''Lake Norman. North of Charlotte. We also took one dive off the coast of Myrtle Beach, in South Carolina.''

Mike would have preferred they have had more than one experience in the ocean, but the shipwreck was relatively safe from potential danger *if* all went well. He told them that, adding, "I'll go over everything after Kelly gets here." He went to where the tanks were for a final check.

Neil hung back, while the others, filled with enthusiasm, went with him. He'd done a lot of thinking since Kelly blew him away, chided himself for having been surprised at her reaction. After all, Verna had told him she had a thing going with the beach bum, and he'd known the odds were stacked against him this time, just as he'd known from the beginning it was going to be an uphill battle all the way to persuade her to marry him. He also knew that most of his attraction to her, anyway, was the fact she'd been such a challenge. He planned to give her one more chance when the dive was over. He'd tell her he was willing to forget the whole escapade if she'd go back with them and promptly announce their engagement. It would be his last effort. After that, to hell with her. He was well aware of his status as one of Charlotte's most eligible bachelors. He could get married any time he wanted.

Kelly was anything but enthused as she doggedly walked across the beach towards the pier. As angry as she was at Neil for showing up, she'd come to the conclusion it was fate telling her to just move on. Edie had found *her* happiness, and Kelly was glad for her, but now she asked herself why should *she* stay? There was no reason, not when it was obviously over with Mike. As for Neil, she cursed herself for having been so stupid as not to have realized before now exactly what had been missing in that relationship, for the ultimate answer was simply—nothing! That's all there was to it. There were no missing pieces. She didn't love him, never would, never could, and that's the way it was.

They were all waiting on the pier. Mike, she noted, didn't look at her as Neil, ever the smug optimist, cheerily greeted, "Hi, honey. Ready to show off everything you've learned?"

She didn't comment, nodded casually to the other three, gave Ronnie a warm smile and went to stand beside him at the helm.

When they were at last on their way, the boat slicing through the water and heading out to sea, Mike told them it would take about ten minutes to get to the dive site. He busied himself checking equipment again. Not once did he glance in Kelly's direction.

At the site, Ronnie killed the engine, proceeded to drop the anchor as Mike gave his usual pre-dive instructions. "As I told you before, the shipwreck is eighty-feet down. The no-decompression limit is forty minutes, but to be on the safe side, I'm allowing you thirty. Explore, see what there is to see, but do not go inside the ship or near the bow because it juts out over a ledge, and sometimes there are dangerous rip currents there. Everybody understand?"

They nodded, acknowledging the possible hazards.

He went on, "Watch me for signals. I've got the depth gauge and watch. Make a note of the colored ribbon on the one you go down on, make sure that's the one you come back up on. Buddy up, and let's get started."

Neil jovially called to Kelly, "Come on, *buddy!*"

Before Kelly could say anything, Mike snapped, "She goes with me."

The others tensed, as Neil shot him an angry look and cracked, "Hey, how about letting *her* decide who she wants to buddy up with, *Romeo!*"

Mike stiffened but managed to hold his temper as

he reminded, "She's not certified yet, Brandon, and according to the rules, she's supposed to buddy with the instructor."

Kelly was losing her patience and whirled on Neil to icily remind, "I thought we settled everything last night."

Indignantly, he fired back, "Yeah, maybe on *your* part, but I didn't get much of a chance to have *my* say, and—"

"Hold it right there!" Mike stepped between them then. "The war stops here or nobody dives."

"Yeah, Neil. You better listen to him," Chad yelled, disgusted. "You talked us into coming down here, saying Kelly wanted to come home, and it was a great opportunity for us to see this shipwreck. You didn't tell us the way it really is. Now if we don't get to dive, we're holding you responsible for the cost of the whole trip."

Larry was quick to agree. "That's right. And it's not fair to the rest of us for you to be acting like a jerk. You two settle your personal problems while we go below."

Kelly began to pull on her face mask. "I don't have any problems, and I'm diving! Nobody is stopping me from getting my certification."

"Are you straight now?" Mike all but shouted at Neil. "Because if you cause any trouble below, so help me, I'll pop your CO_2 cartridge and send you flying straight upwards and into a case of the Bends."

Neil could see by the raging gleam in his eyes that he meant it. "Okay, okay!" He began to yank on his own mask. There'd be time for brooding later, and he wasn't about to be left behind to have to listen to the guys crow on the way home about how great the dive was that *he* didn't get to make.

Chad and Larry buddied, leaving Jay to team with

Neil. Mike motioned everyone to their dive line, and, two by two, on signal, hand over their face masks to protect them, they stepped off the boat and into the water.

Kelly reveled in the sensation of the underwater world that closed about her. Waiting till Mike gripped the line and started descent, she moved behind him. Slowly, they went down, and before long the outline of the wreck was visible. Glancing around, she saw that the others had also reached bottom and were fanning out, marveling at the coral-crusted gunwales, a hatch door half-submerged in the sand. Colorful fish darted about to curiously watch the intruders from above.

Her need to get away from Mike was more compelling than a desire to explore right then, so Kelly began to move away. He signaled for her to return by pointing three fingers of his right hand into the open palm of his left. She pretended not to see, wasn't going far anyway. It was just that being so near him, loving him as she did, was more than she could bear. Knowing, too, that it might be the last time they ever saw each other added to the misery and confusion, and she was wishing she'd foregone this expedition. What difference did it make whether she got her certification? What difference did anything make, anymore, anyway?

She realized the others hadn't stayed buddied up, either, and Mike moved to check on them, deciding she'd stay close by. Chad had an underwater camera and was shooting pictures everywhere. Larry had found the ship's barnacle-crusted anchor and was fascinated. Jay had gone to explore the decks. She couldn't see Neil and didn't care. Gliding along the bottom, Kelly became caught up in the mysterious realm of the deep. Delighting at a variety of sea shells, and then her first sight of a real sea horse, she knew that wherever the future led, she'd have to be near a place to dive. Truly, she had the fever.

Mesmerized, entranced, she lost all track of time, as did the others, and when Mike swam up to her, she could see the anger in his eyes through his mask. He held out his right hand to his side in a fist, the signal to stay where she was. Catching Chad's attention, he raised his arm, indicating to *group up*, then raised two fists together, which meant to *buddy up*.

Kelly realized with a shudder of momentary panic that she'd broken a cardinal rule for a diver with no more experience than she had—she'd lost her perception of exactly where the dive line was located. Remembering her first view of the ship had been from its port side, she calculated she was on starboard, which meant she needed to go around. Though Mike had signaled her to stay put, she felt yet another stab of fear to realize her air was probably running low. Never should they all have fanned out as they did. Mike was using precious time, precious oxygen, to get everyone together to start the ascent. She could save both by going ahead and swimming back to the line.

Turned around and confused, she forgot Mike's warning about staying away from the bow of the ship. Realizing what she'd done, she frantically turned around to go the other way, only to realize Neil was right behind her. His eyes, through his mask, were wild with fear and panic. Pointing at his wrist, then his tank, then forward, she knew he was trying to tell her they were nearly out of air and there wasn't time to go back.

He began to swim, motioned for her to follow, then froze. Directly ahead, at a distance of maybe fifteen feet, a shark was gliding lazily by. It was not headed in their direction, gave no indication of having noticed them, but Neil was terrified. Before Kelly had time to react, he gave her a shove to the side, and she fell backwards, tumbling off the ledge, horrified to realize she was caught in the throes of the rip current Mike had warned about.

Neil saw her swept away, at once decided there was nothing he could do for her without jeopardizing himself and headed for his dive line, commanding himself not to panic in the ascent.

Kelly, whirling over and over, knew terror as never before. Managing to grasp her weight belt, she groped for the buoyancy compensator and popped the CO_2 cartridge. The action was enough to free her from the current, but she was suddenly being violently propelled straight up, with no time for her lungs to decompress.

Ronnie saw her surface about forty feet off the starboard bow, realized she'd come up too fast and was in danger of decompression sickness—*Bends*. He yelled to her to catch the life preserver he quickly threw out, which was attached to the boat by rope, waited to make sure she had hold of it before he rushed in to the radio to fire off an SOS. He then went to each dive line to give a tug, relieved to get a signal in return that meant everyone was on his way up. All he could do then was keep an eye on Kelly and be ready to go in after her if she started losing her grip. He wasn't about to do anything else till Mike surfaced and told him what to do.

Chad and Neil were the first up, with Jay and Larry right behind.

Kelly, meanwhile, was clinging to the preserver but realized she was suddenly starting to feel numb all over, with waves of nausea.

"Get her up, get her up," Neil screamed, starting to yank the rope to pull her in.

Ronnie saw, rushed to knock him away and yelled, "No. Leave her. She's going to have to be taken back down. Bends!"

"*Bends?*" Neil echoed as he stared in horror at Kelly.

Chad spoke up quickly, "Oh, yeah, man, she's sure to have 'em. I saw her when she went up like a rocket. She got caught in the rip current and panicked and popped the cartridge. She could be in bad shape. She has to go down and stay there till the Coast Guard comes to take her to the nearest decompression chamber. Where would that be?" he asked Ronnie.

Ronnie, disgusted, snapped, "In Miami, stupid! Don't you know you never dive unless you know the location of the nearest chamber?"

For one, split second, Neil actually thought about grabbing up a fresh air tank, diving in, and taking her below, but that notion was short-lived as he remembered the awesome sight of the shark. He wasn't about to go down in shark-infested waters and wanted to get the hell out of there as fast as possible and back on dry land.

Just then, Mike surfaced. He didn't have to ask questions. He'd also seen Kelly soaring upwards and surfaced as fast as he dared. As he quickly unfastened his air tank and weight belt, handing them up to Ronnie, he wanted to know, "Did you radio the Coast Guard?" Assured he had, Mike rushed to bark further commands, "Call them back. Tell them I'm taking her down for emergency decompression. Tell them according to the tables for her rate of ascent, I'll need to take her down for at least four hours. Tell them to have a helicopter here then, and a doctor. We'll know by then if she needs airlift to Miami or to the hospital in Nassau. I'm going after her and bring her to the dive line. Get two tanks ready for me. In a half hour, send me two more. And don't forget when I get her within twenty-five of the surface, she'll need to breathe pure oxygen the rest of the way. Have that ready."

Ronnie rushed to obey, and Mike began to swim for Kelly. He could not risk pulling in the rope, for fear she'd lose her hold and slip below. She was still wearing her tank and weight belt.

The others were standing at the railing, and Chad called down, "What can we do?"

Without missing a stroke, Mike gruffly shouted, "Stay out of the way. And tell Ronnie to radio Nassau to send some divers out here to help that know how to obey orders!"

"Screw him," Neil muttered. He'd got himself a can of beer from the cooler he'd brought onboard, tilted it to his lips and drank.

Chad shook his head in pity. "If an air bubble causes a blood clot and reaches her brain, she'll be gone in seconds."

Neil was worried but told himself there was nothing he could do. He described how they'd seen the shark, leaving out how he'd accidently sent Kelly into the rip current. As his friends stared at him with wide, terrified eyes, he pointed out, "Kramer's right. We are in the way. And I say we should get out of here on the first boat bringing out divers. Knowing sharks are around makes me nervous."

The others agreed, all of them anxious to be back on dry land.

Mike, reaching for Kelly, saw at once she was barely conscious. Slipping one arm under her shoulders in the standard rescue grip, he began to swim back towards the boat and dive line. He couldn't have risked having Ronnie move from position, due to the wake of the boat's motor, no matter how low the speed. He offered a silent prayer of thanks for relatively calm seas and good weather. He'd only had to assist in an emergency recompression once before, and it'd been hairy then.

This time, he knew, was going to be even rougher. His heart had a personal stake in this one.

Ronnie had made the calls and returned to lower himself into the water to assist as Mike reached the dive line.

Kelly's eyes were open but glassy. Mike knew she was just before being in real trouble. "Can you hear me?" he asked, touching her cheek, giving her face a gentle shake.

She was barely able to nod her head.

Mike bit back the knot of terror in his throat. It was very important, he knew, for his fear not to show. "Kelly, I want you to listen to me and listen carefully. You came up too fast. Remember all you learned about that. Air embolism is setting in. Pressure is forcing air from the air sacs in your lungs and into your blood vessels. I'm going to take you down and bring you up slowly. You're going to be okay, and I'll be with you the whole time. Don't be scared. Just lean on me, okay?" He forced a smile meant to be reassuring, but she didn't notice, could offer only a weak nod that she understood what he was saying. He repeated to assure, loudly, sternly, "You're going to be okay, Kelly. Trust me."

Ronnie helped to remove Kelly's nearly-empty tank and replaced it with a new one. "Two boats are on the way with divers," he said. "As soon as they get here, I'll be down."

Mike nodded, adjusted his face mask. Making sure Kelly's mouthpiece was in place, he inserted his own. With his arm securely around her waist, he said a silent prayer and began the descent.

SIXTEEN

The sea became her womb, as Kelly's imbalanced body struggled to right itself. When first Mike carried her in descent, she was in the first throes of decompression sickness. She had no perception of the realm around her, for unconsciousness was a hairsbreadth away. Then, as the nitrogen that had dissolved into her bloodstream, caused by the pressure of her rapid ascent, began to desaturate, her mind began to clear. The nausea that had made her stomach heave and roll disappeared, and she was, at last, able to discern the watery world that held her captive.

She recognized Mike, and even through the obscuration of their face masks, could see the intense anxiety mirrored in his cobalt eyes. He had secured her to the dive line, and he held onto it also as they hung suspended above the shipwreck. He pointed to it, then upwards in a fast, swishing motion, indicating what had happened. Releasing his grip on the rope long enough to press both his hands against his chest, he pantomimed her precarious condition, and she was able to nod that she understood.

Through the clouds that still shrouded her mind, it was all struggling to come back to her, and she shuddered to realize what she'd so stupidly done in panic. Yet, what other choice did she have? The rip current could have held her imprisoned till her air supply was exhausted, and she'd have drowned. What was slowly, but insidiously dawning to inspire anger was remembering it was *Neil's* hysteria that had caused her dilemma, not her own.

Gesturing upwards in successive motion, she meant to convey her question as to how long before they would surface. When Mike held up four fingers, she groaned inside. She had to remain below for that many hours. Exhausted, she felt herself drifting away, lulled by the ethereal surroundings.

Amidst the pain in her chest, and the hazy, murky way her mind drifted in and out of consciousness, Kelly knew what was meant by the saying that a drowning person's life flashes before them. All the way back, she went in time, reliving doubts and fears and hopes and ambitions.

She'd been accused of rebellion, though wasn't it actually revenge? Her mother had mapped out her life, but Kelly had not conformed. Her acts of defiance were, in fact, punishment for anyone who'd dare attempt to control her life. No matter whether she be thought right or wrong, it had been her defense mechanism, as natural as the breathing she'd taken for granted—till now, when death could so easily sweep her away.

Admittedly, the decision to change from pre-med to instead study veterinary medicine had been motivated by the subconscious knowledge that her mother wouldn't like it. But she'd excelled, had, quite by accident, discovered her own true calling. She *loved* her work.

Len's face swam before her, distorted amidst the current, blurred within the rainbow flickers of passing sea life. Truly, he'd been an act of self-destruction as she unknowingly punished herself for having hurt and disappointed her parents when she switched studies. Now she could rationalize it had not been necessary, any of it. She owed no apologies for charting her own course in life!

Neil, she knew now, grimacing at his murky image before her, never had a chance in her heart. He'd been merely an interlude, another subconscious act, this time yet another needless offer of atonement to her parents for past disobedience.

Mike had seen how her face contorted, as though in pain, and he reached out to touch her. She managed a wan smile, then lapsed into her chimerical illusion once more.

In her subliminal mind, she knew she loved Mike beyond all doubt, just as she could acknowledge that for the first time in her life she'd not been rebelling against anything. The past weeks she'd been doing what she enjoyed, with no thought as to whether anyone else approved or disapproved. There was no revenge, no disobedience. Yet, she was all too painfully aware it might be too late to reap the glory of her new self-awareness.

Ronnie descended with three other divers. He had also brought an underwater slate, on which he scribbled to communicate that the Coast Guard was waiting above, as well as a doctor. He was ready to take Mike's place for awhile. Mike shook his head, not about to leave Kelly to anyone else's care.

It was an errie world Kelly awoke to when next she regained consciousness. Instead of only one face anxiously staring at her through a rubber and plastic mask, she saw five. Mike scribbled on the slate to ask if she felt dizzy. She shook her head. He asked if she felt numb. Again, she indicated negatively. *"You're going to be o.k.,"* he wrote, and she managed another pasty smile around her mouthpiece. Erasing his words, he then scrawled, *"Half-way. Two more hours."* This time, she was able to grin.

Divers came and went, but Mike remained constant. He could tell Kelly was exhausted but dared to hope she was well on the way to being decompressed and that the danger was just about over. As he held her, he experienced pain of his own to acknowledge it might be for the last time. As much as he loved her, adored her, never would he approach her without encouragement. When this was over, she would, of course, be grateful for his having helped save her life, but he didn't want her to think he might expect something in return—like commitment. Though he wanted that, and much, much more, they could have no future unless she freely returned his love. All he could do was wait for her to make the next move once the crisis was over.

Things happened fast after the last hour at twenty-five feet below the surface. Kelly was only vaguely aware when she was, at last, lifted out of the water and onto the Coast Guard cutter. She was not aware of Edie watching from nearby, standing at the bow of Burt's boat, his arms around her in comfort as fearful tears streamed down her cheeks. Neither did she know that, as the doctor checked her vital signs, Mike was also being examined for any ill effects from having been submerged so long. But he wasn't cooperating, refusing to be still as he strained to hear what the doctor was saying about her.

Confidently, he announced, "She should be okay. No need to take her into Miami. She doesn't need the chamber, but she does need to get to the Nassau hospital as fast as possible for precautionary treatment—anti-platelets, hydrocortisone to head off any effect on the central nervous system.'' He started intravenous fluid as there were signs of slight dehydration.

She was unaware of being air-lifted to Nassau by helicopter, and the rest of that day, and the next, passed in an exhausted blur. When, at last, she awoke, Edie's was the first face she saw, staring anxiously from her vigil at the foot of the bed. Kelly glanced around, wanting to know where she was, and then it all came flooding back at once.

After they'd talked about all that had happened, Edie assured, ''The doctor says you're fine. He wanted you to rest, and you have, and now I'm going to have them bring you something to eat.''

Kelly was ravenously hungry and devoured everything on the tray. As she ate, she asked who had sent all the flowers that seemed to be everywhere.

''Your folks sent one—''

''You called them?''

''Of course, I did. They needed to know, and . . .'' Edie hastened to sharply add, ''I let Verna know what I thought of her little scheme. She broke down and cried, apologizing all over the place, and Walter was on the phone, and it seemed he didn't know anything about any of it, and he was furious with her. She said to tell you she really means it this time—that she's not going to interfere in your life ever again, and she wants you to call her when you're up to it, so she can tell you that.''

Kelly nodded perfunctorily. ''I will. I've got some things to say to her, too.''

Edie raised an eyebrow. ''Such as?''

''Such as how I realized a lot down there, and I don't intend ever again to apologize for being in control of my own life!''

Edie clapped her hands in delight. ''Good girl!''

Kelly glanced at the other four floral arrangements,

hoping one of them was from Mike. "Who sent those?"

"Dr. Brewster, Anna and Winny, me and Burt, and . . ." she paused, knowing what Kelly was hoping and hating to disappoint her, "the big one there is from Neil. It came in with the one from your folks."

Kelly nodded resolutely. It was silly to expect flowers from Mike when they'd broken up. Besides, she should be sending some to him for helping save her life.

Edie continued in an angry rush, "I should keep my opinion to myself, but frankly, I think Neil Brandon is a wimp. Anna told me that Ronnie told her that when the first boat arrived at the dive site bringing more divers, Neil and his friends paid to get back to Harbour Island. They probably flew home that afternoon."

"Good," Kelly nodded vigorously, "because if he'd dared to show his face, I'd clobber him." She proceeded to tell how Neil was the one who caused her to be trapped in the rip current.

Edie wasn't surprised, said she'd never trusted him, anyway. Then, almost cautiously, she wanted to know, "Can I tell you something else, Kelly? Something I've never told anybody?"

Puzzled, she assured, "You know you can."

Taking a deep breath, Edie began. "I married your grandfather because he was rich. I knew at the time I didn't love him the way I'd always hoped I'd love the man I married, but my parents were pushing me, telling me I'd live a life of luxury. I did, but I also lived a life of misery that no one knew about but me because I hated to let everyone know how stupid I'd been.

"To be perfectly honest," she went on, looking a bit ashamed to admit, "the years since he died have been the happiest of my life—till now." Her face suddenly exploded with radiance. "For the first time, I know what it is to really and truly love somebody the way God intended.''

Kelly pushed her tray aside, held out her arms and they embraced, both crying with mutual joy, and then Kelly wanted to know, ''But why are you telling me all this now? You don't have to justify wanting to marry Burt to me. You know I'm happy for both of you.''

''Because . . .'' Edie stepped back, wiped at her eyes as she soberly informed, ''I don't want you to make the same mistake I did. I know I said I wasn't going to give you any more advice, but I just felt like maybe it would help you to know about my sad experience in case the only thing holding you back where Mike is concerned is the fact that he is somewhat of a vagabond, and—''

''Have you ever heard of Neptune, Incorporated?'' Kelly interrupted to ask, smiling mysteriously.

Edie's eyes narrowed thoughtfully. ''I . . . I don't think so,'' she shook her head, then wanted to know, ''What's that got to do with anything?''

''Neptune, Incorporated, is a chain of dive shops in the Bahamas. A very *profitable* chain, I might add. Mike happens to own it.''

Edie gasped. ''When did he tell you that?''

''He hasn't. I found it out myself. Don't you see?'' She pushed back the covers, sat up, and swung around to perch on the side of the bed as she went on to explain, ''He didn't want me to know he's well off financially. He wanted me to *see* him, *love* him, for *himself*.''

Edie quickly wanted to know, ''And do you?''

''Yes,'' she firmly avowed, ''I do, but I didn't realize that till I was down there, in the water all that time, and all the revelations came to me, and now I see things like they really are, why I've done the things I have in the past. I've got all that together now, and it's a good feeling. As for Mike, I don't care if he's rich or poor, and, oh, Edie, don't you see?'' She reached to clasp her hands. ''You didn't even have to tell me about your own tragedy with Grandpa. I'm sorry it was like that, and I'm just glad you're going to have true happiness, at last, with Burt, but I know now that the most important thing in life is to be willing to pay any price when you love someone. It doesn't matter what anyone else thinks because you just can't rely on other people. You have to rely on yourself. I *do* love Mike, and I'm willing to take a chance on what I feel for him.

''So what if there are problems?'' She got out of bed then, began to walk slowly around the room, relieved she felt no weakness. ''Even if being in love does screw up your life, so what? If it's good, it's worth it, and isn't the bottom line here that if you aren't willing to take the chance, life isn't worth living, anyway?''

Slyly, with eyes twinkling, Edie asked, ''You mean—like daring to go for the brass ring?''

''Exactly!'' She whirled about to face her then, waving her arms in wild jubilation. ''And as for Mom and Dad, maybe I don't *like* them, but I'll always *love* them, and I'm going to keep that thought from now on when they try to drive me up a wall, and I'll react accordingly—with tolerance and understanding instead of anger or rebellion, or, worse, *revenge!* And . . .'' her voice trailed as she saw the way Edie was looking at her—sympathetic, pitying. Alarmed, she asked, ''What is it? What's wrong? Aren't you glad I've finally seen the light?'' She gave a nervous laugh.

''Of course, I am,'' Edie sternly assured. ''It's just that before the accident, you said you and Mike were through, and I know his quick action is what saved your life and that he never left your side for a minute, but the fact is, you've been here since the day before yesterday, and he hasn't been here.''

Kelly felt a chilling stab of awareness. There was still the matter to settle of his thinking she'd lied about her involvement with Neil, and, with painful clarity, she remembered his angry accusation she'd never really loved him. Mike had his pride, but, by golly, she wasn't giving up. "Can you get me some clothes?" she suddenly asked.

Edie shook her head doubtfully. "I'm not sure the doctor is ready to discharge you. When he made his rounds this morning while you were still sleeping, he said he thought it might be best if you just took it easy awhile, and—"

"Nonsense. Where's my swimsuit?"

"If you mean the bikini you were wearing when they brought you in, a nurse gave it to me after they put that hospital gown on you, and I hung it in the shower stall to dry, and—" She fell silent, watched as Kelly hurried into the bathroom.

When she returned, she was wearing the bikini, and Edie promptly gasped, "Where do you think you're going?"

"Harbour Island. Let's go."

Baffled, bewildered, Edie had no choice but to follow along as Kelly walked briskly past the nurse's station, all eyes staring. It was not a common sight to see a girl in a string bikini, barefooted, going down the hall.

They took a taxi to the waterfront, where they quickly got passage to the island. Edie settled back, amused, and glad that, at long last, Kelly was asserting herself, albeit going a bit overboard!

When they reached Dunmore Town harbor, Kelly was disappointed not to see the *Free Spirit* at the dock. She did, however, spot Burt, who anxiously hurried over when he saw them. "Do you know where Mike is?" she wanted to know.

With his arm around Edie, he replied, "He took a dive group out to the shipwreck."

"Will you take me there? Now?" she pleaded.

He looked around from her, to Edie, who was imploring him with her eyes to cooperate. With a sigh and a shrug he agreed, but, as soon as he could get Edie to one side, he wanted to know what on earth was going on. She gave him a mischievous wink, a secretive smile, and chirped, "She's going for the brass ring!"

Ronnie waved as Burt pulled up gently alongside Mike's boat. "You okay now?" he greeted Kelly anxiously when she stepped onboard. She assured him she was, immediately wanting to know how long the dive team had been down. "Only five minutes," he said, glancing at his watch.

"Help me with a tank, and get me the underwater slate."

Ronnie, Edie, and Burt all watched in quiet amusement as Kelly adjusted the harness to the air tank, her weight belt, and mouth piece, then took a giant sidestep off the boat and into the water.

Following one of the dive lines, she made her descent, finally reaching the hulking shadow of the shipwreck. Glancing about, she saw a diver, swam over to him and signaled with her hands to ask where the dive master was. He pointed, and she went in that direction to recognize Mike where he usually liked to position himself to keep an eye on all the divers in his care.

His back was to her. She paused, scribbled her message on the slateboard, then swam over to him to tap him on his shoulder as she prayed it wasn't too late.

Turning, he jumped in surprise. The last place he'd expected to see her was eighty feet below.

She held out the slate.

He took it, bewildered, then read her tersely written avowal: *"Your world, my world."*

Struggling to keep from choking as he fought back joyous laughter, he took the waterproof chalk from her, and, after erasing her message, proceeded to quickly write one of his own: *"Our world. I love you."*

She reached for the slate to communicate her love for him, as well, but he let it go, and, as it gently floated towards the surface, he reached for her to pull her tightly into his arms. With hindrance of mouthpiece and face masks, a kiss of love avowed was impossible.

But they had what was most important for the moment—they had . . . *a touch of love*.

SHARE THE FUN . . .
SHARE YOUR NEW-FOUND TREASURE!!

You don't want to let your new books out of your sight? That's okay. Your friends can get their own. Order below.

No. 7 SILENT ENCHANTMENT by Lacey Dancer
She was elusive and beautiful. She was Alex's true-to-life princess.

No. 29 FOSTER LOVE by Janis Reams Hudson
Morgan comes home to claim his children and finds Sarah who claims his heart.

No. 30 REMEMBER THE NIGHT by Sally Falcon
Levelheaded Joanna throws caution to the wind and finds Nathan just isn't her fantasy but her reality as well.

No. 32 SWEET LAND OF LIBERTY by Ellen Kelly
Brock has a secret and Liberty's freedom could be in serious jeopardy!

No. 33 A TOUCH OF LOVE by Patricia Hagan
Kelly seeks peace and quiet and finds paradise in Mike's arms.

No. 34 NO EASY TASK by Chloe Summers
Hunter is wary when Doone delivers a package that will change his life.

No. 35 DIAMOND ON ICE by Lacey Dancer
Diana could melt even the coldest of hearts. Jason hasn't a chance.

No. 36 DADDY'S GIRL by Janice Kaiser
Slade wants more than Andrea is willing to give. Who wins?